The Hunt for R. L. Nox
An Ed and Mel Decodable Adventure

Heather Doolittle

The characters and events in this book are fictitious. Any similarity to real persons, living or dead, or actual events is purely coincidental and not intended by the author.

DecodableAdventures.com

ISBN-13: 979-8-6370-0779-0

To DN, AP, and KR.
Thank you for your help with this book.
Your hard work is an inspiration.

Forward

As a parent of a dyslexic student, I know how important it is to help students find their strengths as they work through their weaknesses caused by dyslexia interacting with their environment. There are many ways to encourage and support our students as they explore their strengths. It is important for students to know that they are more than just their struggles.

I also think it is important to remember that it takes time to find one's strengths and develop them. That is a journey all of its own. In *The Hunt for R. L. Nox*, Ed and Mel must draw on their developing strengths as they hunt down R. L. They find it isn't always so easy.

As we each develop our strengths, we need to matter, not when success is reached or failure avoided, but now. We all need a caring community, acceptance, support, and love in the middle of the mess. Strength comes from more than just one's abilities and successes.

The Hunt for R. L. Nox is inspired by my family's experiences with dyslexia. It is designed to be read by the student AND the parent or tutor— in other words— in community. The parent or tutor has the honor of supporting the student and being on their team. The narrator passages are for the parent or tutor to read, the student will read the student text, and the games are for everyone to play.

Skills are added to the student text as the story progresses. The student text follows the Level 4 Barton Reading & Spelling scope and sequence closely. Notes will help the parent or tutor know which skills are being added to the student reading passage and games. Variations from the Barton scope and sequence are minor and will be noted. This book may also be used with other Orton-Gillingham inspired programs or phonics programs. It can be read when a student has completed Barton Reading & Spelling Level 4, or portions of it can be read as the student progresses through Level 4.

Before you start reading, here are a few tips to help maximize the learning opportunities provided in the book. First, take the time to discuss the vocabulary in the "Narrator" text. Building a student's vocabulary will help build their background knowledge and reading comprehension skills. If you find a word of which you are not sure of the meaning, look it up with your student. This is a great opportunity to model this habit for your student.

Also, as a chapter book, the only starting and stopping points are where a bookmark is placed. A bookmark is a great symbol of recognizing the need to end an activity with the anticipation of picking it up again at a later time. Have your student pick out a bookmark before starting *The Hunt for R. L. Nox*. It may be a great signal for your student to use to say, "I need a break. I will start again later."

Chapter 1

Required skills for student text:

Open syllables or long vowel sounds of a, e, i, o, u in open syllables. "Y" at the end of a word read as long I.

Sight words: put, how, both, walk, once, none, two, pull, now, know, their, her, these, come

Barton Level: **Level 4 lesson 1**.

Notes for the book:
Suffix "s" and suffix "ing" are used throughout the book. As suffixes, they are out of sequence from Barton Reading & Spelling Level 4, but they are decodable where used. These words are intended for reading practice only.

There is an occasional use of apostrophe + s for a possessive noun. i.e. Jax's, Mel's, Henry's

Narrator (Parent or Tutor):

Dear Reader,

Sometimes life is ironic. We get the opposite of what is expected. Less is more. Strength from weakness. Failure moving someone towards success. The unexpected.

R. L. Nox's plans to gain riches, fame, and power have taken an ironic turn. The very steps he took to ensure nothing went wrong with his plans actually helped create the very thing that is messing up all his plans.

R. L.'s plans began when he was introduced to the legend of *The Black Silk Path*. No one thought the legend was true, but R. L. looked further into the stories and began to think differently. He suspected that Ebrin, the other world that lay beyond The Black Silk Path, was real. In the legends Ebrin was described as a place of untold riches and creativity. Even the roads were lined

1

with gold and diamonds. Feats of engineering and creativity helped the citizens of Ebrin live prosperous and full lives. The Black Silk Path provided a way into Ebrin, and R. L. was going to find it. He had big dreams of what he could do if he could gain access to the riches of Ebrin. R. L. just needed a little help navigating the clues and travel.

This is where Mr. and Mrs. Davis came in. R. L. needed their help. The Davises were seasoned world travelers. Their expertise in exploration and world cultures were just what he needed to find and navigate The Black Silk Path. At first, he offered to share the wealth of Ebrin, but Mr. Davis compared his plan to theft or larceny. R. L. wasn't bothered. The comparison was accurate. R. L. also wasn't bothered with kidnapping Mr. and Mrs. Davis to force them to help him. To ensure that the Davis couple would help him, he placed a spell on the Davis children, Ed and Mel. Of course, he told Mr. and Mrs. Davis he would remove the spell from Ed and Mel after they helped him. This spell stole Ed and Mel's ability to communicate with words. They wouldn't be able to help themselves order a hamburger much less lead a search for their parents. The Davis couple would make sure he found Ebrin. The spell on the kids would keep them out of the way and make sure that Mr. and Mrs. Davis would cooperate. This would ensure nothing went wrong, or that is what R. L. expected.

R. L. didn't expect what actually happened. At first R. L.'s plan was going well. He was positioned in a good place to start moving goods out of Ebrin when the Davis children showed up and rescued their parents. R. L. could have dealt with losing the Davis couple at this point if they had just crawled back home. But things took a turn for the worse. First, Mr. and Mrs. Davis told the Ebrinites of his intentions to steal everything he could. Second, the spell that should have disabled Ed and Mel didn't quite stop them. It actually made them very determined to stop him and his plans. R. L. had to leave his base of operations and change his plans or be captured by the Davises.

R. L. did not expect to be on the run, hunted by the Davises. He was quite irritated. He just wanted to focus on his plans to gain the riches of Ebrin. After he was rich, he could live a life of luxury and fame back in his own world. But now, he was on the run hastily planning smash and grab robberies throughout Ebrin. He was determined to become rich whether the Davis clan was after him or not. He would not be stopped even if he had to resort to more unpleasant tactics to reach his goal.

It is true that the spell helped inspire Ed and Mel Davis to stop R. L. Nox. They want to stop the man who has caused them so much trouble by kidnapping their parents and stealing their ability to communicate. They have felt the pain of not having their parents and the frustration of not being able to read, write, or speak. They understand that R. L. only cares for himself. They don't want others to be hurt by his evil plans.

The day R. L. Nox stole Ed and Mel's parents and placed the spell on Ed and Mel, their whole lives changed. Instead of exploring the world with their parents, they found themselves alone and unable to speak. First, they had to find a way to communicate. They couldn't even tell anyone that their parents were missing. They had tried multiple things to help, but the only thing that did anything was learning how to read again. It wasn't easy, but as Ed and Mel began to relearn sounds, letters, and how to blend them into words, they could speak those words. The more they could read, the more they could say.

Finally, Ed and Mel were able to try to tell the authorities about their missing parents, but they weren't well understood. They were almost locked up in an orphanage for orphaned and disadvantaged children. That is when they decided they had to find their parents on their own.

They followed clues and found The Black Silk Path and Ebrin. That is when Jax found them. Jax had met Ed and Mel's parents through the window of a locked shed. He promised them he would watch for Ed and Mel.

Together Ed, Mel, and Jax rescued Mr. and Mrs. Davis. Jax soon became a close friend and ally. Once they all learned of R. L.'s greedy plans, they knew they had to stop him. The Davis family knew more about R. L., his plans, and his world than anyone else. Ebrin needed their help.

So Ed, Mel, their parents, and Jax started the hunt for R. L. Nox. They have been looking through R. L.'s rented house looking for clues to his whereabouts. In fact, they are there finishing up now.

Student text:

"Watch it!" Jax did yell. A small stack of texts fell on Jax's hand.

"Are you O.K.? I didn't know that they would fall. My bad," said Ed. "This spot is a mess. R. L. has so much in this den. Do you think we have all the stuff that will help us find R. L.?"

"Let's put all the stuff on the bench and scan the stash," Mel said as she flung junk off the bench.

Mom put a scroll on the bench. Dad put a map of their land and one of Jax's land on the bench. Mel put a list of spots from the maps next to the scroll. Jax did pick up a small chunk of gold and put it on the bench. It had dots in a band on its rim. The band of dots did twist and roll on the gold.

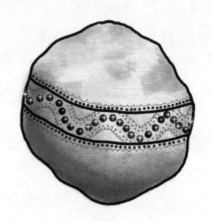

Ed put a small box on the bench. He put his box with a shell that did match it next to it.

The last thing to go on the bench was a big block. It was in a box which could have held two of them. One block was not there. This block was black. It had a small bump on the top. The rest of it was flat and slick. By the bump on the top it said, "Roll one block to cast a spell. Roll two blocks and the spell will last."

The small gang did step back to scan the bench. As they did scan the stash of stuff, Ash ran and did jump up on Mel. Ash was a fluff ball who did find Ed and Mel when they got to this long-lost land of The Black Silk Path. He had the mass of a cat, but he was not long and thin as a cat. He was a ball of fluff. Ash went where Mel went. If Mel was there, so was Ash.

Jax did rub his hand and said, "I did draft and craft that map. I know that stretch of land. My best bet is that R. L. went to that spot there. I know that bit of gold on the bench is from that spot on the map."

Mom said, "If I squint at the maps, I can spot small dots of ink. Both maps have twin dots. If we put one on the top of the...

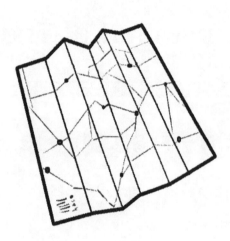

yes! They do match! These dots match spots in this land to the land we are from. What do you think that will tell us?

Ed did spot a rock on one map. It was the rock where they got on the Black Silk Path. It did match up to the spot where he and Mel did pop in to this land. He said, "I think these dots match up where there is a rift, a crack with a path from one land to the next. You know, a spot to get from one land to the next."

"How many are there?" Dad did ask.

"Six," Jax said. "There are six that match up. So, six spots to get on The Black Silk Path and six spots to get off the path." "R. L. can get back to the land he is from. He has the shell to get him on the path. We can't stall," said Mel. "Bring it all with us. The scroll and the list will have to be put on hold. R. L. still has one black block to cast a spell. We must be quick."

Game to play: The Hunt is On

Ed, Mel, Jax, Mom, and Dad need to go after R. L. Nox. Collect the six items on the bench. Then, leave R. L.'s house through the door.

Materials needed:

- A game token for each player.
- Six small markers for each player, such as transparent color counting chips.
- One six-sided die.
- Game board and game cards. See Game Appendix.

Rules:

<u>Phase One:</u>

1. Roll the die. Move to the number rolled on the die. The numbered spaces are in the box. Place a counting chip or small marker on that same number in the player's score box.
2. Draw a card and read the word.
   a. If the word is an open syllable, place an additional counting chip on any number in the player's score box. The player will place a total of two counting chips. One counting chip is placed for the roll of the die, and one is placed for drawing an open syllable word.
   b. If the word is not an open syllable, it is now Player Two's turn. Only one counting chip is placed for the dice roll when a closed syllable is drawn.

c. If a counting chip has already been played on the number where the player lands and the player does not have an open syllable word to place an extra chip, the player's turn is over without putting a chip in the score box.

3. Players must place a counting chip on all six numbers in their score box to collect all six items. Once all six items have been collected, a player can move on to play Phase Two. A player does not have to wait for the other players to finish phase one before moving on to phase two.

Phase Two:

1. Pick a card and read it. If the word is read correctly, roll the die. Move that number of spaces along the path towards the door. The player's turn is over.

2. Once a player is close to the door, they must roll the exact number to land on the door. If a player's roll would put them past the door, they may not move from the die roll. If the card they read before rolling the die is an open syllable word, they may move one space closer to the door.

3. First player to "open" the door at the end wins the game.

Note for game boards and game cards in the book: On some game boards, keeping track of points directly on the game board will make it a one-time use game. To be able to replay the game without making lots of copies of the game board, put the game board in a page protector or laminate it to use with a dry erase marker. Sticky notes in the player's points box or a separate piece of paper may also be used to keep score. Another option is to place and remove counter type tokens in the player's points box to keep track of the points. A link to printable game boards and game cards can be found on the "eBook users" page at DecodableAdventures.com.

Chapter 2

Additional required skills for student text:

Ability to read two syllable words using the syllable division rule for one consonant between the vowels. (dividing vcv) "Y" at the end of the word read as long E.

Barton Level: **Level 4 Lesson 2**.

Note: ASAP is in the student text and is to be read as "as soon as possible" or with the first syllable as an open syllable and the second as a closed syllable, A-SAP. It can also be read by naming each of the letter names.

Narrator (Parent or Tutor):

The Davis clan, Jax, and Ash all headed out towards the area Jax recognized on the map. As he mentioned, Jax had drawn the map they found in R. L.'s house. It was his creative contribution to Ebrin. Ebrinites placed a high value on creativity. Everyone used their unique gifts to create something, whether that was maps, mathematical equations, or the arts and crafts that filled the cities and villages. Someone like R. L. would put the most value on the precious metals and jewels the Ebrinites used for their art. The Ebrinites valued the creativity more than the gold or jewels. Jax knew the area on his map well. He had an idea where R. L. was headed.

As they traveled, Mom and Dad helped Ed and Mel review their reading lessons. They needed to continue to fight the spell R. L. Nox placed upon them. Mel was so relieved to learn about open syllables. She got so tired of saying "you and I" all the time instead of "we." It was also helpful to learn about multiple syllable words and syllable division. It was a lot of work trying to find all the right one-syllable words to communicate what she wanted.

At first Ed kept forgetting which direction to move when there was just one consonant placed between two vowels, so he made up a game to help him remember to try the consonant with the end syllable *first*. Learning to read and speak again was a lot of work, but it was worth it.

Mom was excited for Ed and Mel too. But as moms can do, Mom worried about the spell on Ed and Mel. How was Mel going to become the vet she dreamed about being if she couldn't read well? How was Ed going to become the leader she could see in him if he couldn't communicate with others well?

Mom said, "Ed, Mel. I am so sorry that R. L. placed this spell on you two. I feel like it is Dad's and my fault for not stopping R. L. in the first place." Tears welled up in her eyes. "I'm just so sorry that it is so hard to read and speak again."

Now that confused Jax a bit. He said, "So, why are you so sad that it takes so much work to learn to read? It seems to me like it is perfectly normal to have trouble learning to read."

Mom looked surprised, so Jax explained, "You see, in Ebrin, creative and out of the box thinking is normal. It comes naturally. The skills required for reading easily are not natural. Most Ebrinites have to work really hard at reading skills. Reading is difficult to learn. In fact, those who do learn to read quickly and easily are often identified at school as needing extra help in the creative arts. Ebrinites recognize everyone has their own strengths, even if they don't fit the normal Ebrinite strengths. We support and encourage each other. It is okay if some aren't as creative as the others. Each person has a strength to contribute to Ebrin."

Student text:

"Mom," said Mel, "R. L. put this spell on us. You didn't put it on us. As Jax said, all kids have a skill with which they can help. Ed and I have skills and grit. We will not stop. We will end this spell. We will even stop this thug, R. L. Nox. Don't focus on the bad. We have a lot of spunk. We will study, and we will focus on the skills we have to get things done."

Jax said, "That's it! Focus on what you do well. If you do your best with your skills, then all of us will profit. We all help and finish the job."

Mom said, "I will shift my habit to think

of the skills you have and not the ones you don't. Thank you, Mel." She said to Jax, "Thank you, Jax. This will help me to not be sad with the spell on Ed and Mel. I wish the land we are from would do this as well as Ebrin does."

All at once Ed and Dad did gasp. Ed did yell, "I spy a…umm…umm…a wisp of black from the land up to the sky. What could that be?"

They all spun to the front of the path to spy the totem of black that did stretch up to the sky.

"No, no, no!" Jax did yell back. "It can't be. The tiny city of Jalisp is in crisis. What did R. L. do?! We must get there now!"

The small band began to run. They had to help Jalisp and catch R. L. Nox. They had to get there ASAP.

Game to play: Ed's Syllable Division Game

Play the game Ed made to help him remember how to use the first syllable division rule he and Mel learned.

Materials needed:
- Game board and game cards. See Game Appendix.

Rules:
1. Draw a card.
2. Divide the word.

   The player gains a point if they try the consonant in the middle of the vowels to the end syllable **first**. Even if the player knows the word, they will read the first syllable as an open syllable and then read the second syllable. If it doesn't make a real word, they will move the consonant in the middle of the vowels to the beginning syllable.

   The player earns a second point if the word is divided with the consonant going to the end syllable. If the consonant does divide to the first syllable (first syllable is closed), the player does not earn an extra point. This is to emphasize dividing a VCV word the most common way the first time. Ed really wants to remember to try the consonant to the end first.
3. The player who earns the most points wins the game.

Chapter 3

Additional required skills for student text:

Ability to read two syllable words using the syllable division rule for two consonants between the vowels. (dividing vccv)

Barton Level: **Level 4 Lesson 3**

Narrator (Parent or Tutor):

As the Davises, Jax, and frisky Ash reached Jalisp, it became clear that something was very wrong. They could see black smoke pouring out from the meeting hall. No one was there to fight the flames. In fact, no one was there at all. The only sign of life were a few scared and jumpy animals hitched to empty carts or tied to lamp posts. The city had been torn apart. Broken glass, crushed boxes, and random items dotted the streets. Open doors slowly swung back and forth in the light breeze. Mel shuddered as a deep sense of dread settled upon the group. No one spoke as they surveyed the damage. Mel broke the silence as she ran to free the horse-like animals from their carts.

Student text:

"Mom, Dad, help me unhitch this sad baby from the post. Ed and Jax, help that one there," Mel began to direct.

"Mel, we will put them in the pen next to the hotel, and then we must find the Jalisp kin," Jax said.

"Yes, that pen will be a decent spot for them. That should help them rest and protect them. They must have a drink and a bit of grub too. Then we can find the Jalisp kin," Mel said.

Ed got the pen all set. He did want to help, but he did not want to get next to a thing with fuzz. He did not want to be next to a thing with fangs. He would not be their lunch if he was not next to them.

Once they did finish Mel's task, they began their hunt for the Jalisp kin. They went from spot to spot checking for them. Ed did pry open a lock. Jax did pry some open too.

"What if they are not in the city?" Dad did ask.

"I just have a strong hunch that they are in the city still," Jax said.

"I trust your gut, Jax," said Mel. "We will not stop hunting."

"Where could they be? We did check so many spots. I don't think it would help to check them again," Mom did add.

"Let's stop and think. We did check the dwellings, shops, sheds, and the grand hall. No one is there. R. L. must be behind this. What would he do?" Dad said.

"That nasty man would have cast a spell," Mel stated.

Ed did grab his pack and did pull the black block from it. He set it in front of Mel. She did focus on the object. She did detect a small flash from the bump on the top.

"This block wasn't blinking when it was on the bench. Let's walk the city with this. We don't know, but it could help," Mel said.

"Let's try it. It is the one plan we have,"

said Jax. "Thank you."

As they went along, Mel kept her focus on the black block. The rest did scan the city again for the Jalisp kin. As they got next to the dentist and vet duplex, the black block began to blink red. They all did stop.

Ash began to sniff. He did detect a smell and began to yap and yelp. Mel went to pick him up but couldn't. He was so spunky that she did drop the block as she bent to get him.

The block did roll to a stop in the mud. It began to hum and thump. Ash hid behind Mel. They all felt their skin begin to sting. The sky was getting dim. Then a shrill cry did erupt from the duplex.

Game to play: Syllable Hunt

Before they were hunting for the Jalisp kin, Ed and Mel were hunting to find the syllables in words. Use your syllable division rules to hunt for the syllables that make up the word on your card.

Materials needed:
- Game board and game cards. See Game Appendix.
- Two different colors of plastic counting chips (or other markers), 24 for each player.

Rules:
1. Draw a card.
2. Divide the word into its 2 syllables.
3. Find each syllable on the game board and place a counting chip on those squares.
4. It is the next player's turn.
5. The first player to get four counting chips in a row wins the game. If neither player gets four counting chips in a row, the player who has the most rows of three counting chips wins. Rows can be horizontal, vertical, or diagonal.

Chapter 4

Additional required skills for student text:

No new reading skills.

Sight words: very, sure, mother, brother, only, push, nothing, about, because, father, friend, full, busy, love

Barton Level: **Level 4 Lesson 4**.

Note: The word "sorry" is used in this chapter. It is underlined. "Sorry" is used as a sight word out of sequence from the Barton Reading & Spelling System scope and sequence.

Narrator (Parent or Tutor):

The deafening noise forced Ed, Mel, their parents, and Jax to cover their ears. Then it suddenly stopped. Jax looked around and saw a Jalisp citizen slowly open the dentist office door. Soon, the whole town slowly stumbled out of various buildings. They were dazed and in shock. The spell that R. L. placed on them had suspended them between realms. They were neither in Ebrin nor in Ed and Mel's world. The in-between was like a bad dream from which they couldn't awaken. They could see their rescuers, but their cries for help couldn't be heard. When Mel dropped the black spell block, it reopened the path to Ebrin.

The people of Jalisp were not well. They had several wounded citizens, and those who weren't wounded were still a little disoriented from the spell. They were also devastated to see their city in ruins. Their art, buildings, and even roads had been crudely dismantled so that R. L. Nox could get the jewels, gold, and other precious metals.

As the people gathered, Mom and Dad started setting up a first aid station for the wounded. Ed and Mel began setting up places for people to sit. People recognized Jax and gave him hugs. They started to process and share what had happened.

Student text:

A child, Henry, ran to Jax and began to cry. "That bad man did mess up the city. What he left is now junk. Why did he do this Jax?"

Jax did grab Henry to hug him. "R. L. Nox is a bad man. He does want all the gold and things for himself. My friend Ed and my friend Mel will help us catch R. L. Nox. We will stop him. We will help the city." Jax did grin at Mel.

Henry did thank Ed and Mel for the help. He did grab Mel's hand and did pull her to his mom.

"Mom!" said Henry. "Mom, this is Mel.

She will help catch the bad man. She is my hero. Ed will help too. He is my hero too."

"Ed is my brother," said Mel. "It is . . . well, I am happy to . . . umm, umm, <u>sorry</u>. I am happy to get to know you."

"Don't be <u>sorry</u>, Mel. I am happy to get to know you too," Henry's mom said. "Thank you for helping Henry. His panic about the bad man is less now. So, you are not from Ebrin? Tell me about your land." Mel and Henry's mom did chat for a bit.

Ed and Jax were both busy picking up rubbish and fixing up some of the shops with some men.

"Ed. Jax," a man who went by David

said. "Help me lift this plank up off the well. We have to put some wet stuff on the grand hall. There won't be much of the hall left, but it will help stop the smog in the sky."

They did help lift the plank and stop the smog. The hall was all ash when they were done.

When Ed, Jax, and Mel met Mom and Dad, a small camp had been set up. A potluck was set up on one end of the camp.

Ed, Mel, and Jax did munch some grits. Ed and Mel sat on a blanket and did spy the Jalisp kin as they did help their friends.

Mel did watch Jax help Henry and his Mom.

Mel said to Ed, "I think I love the land of Ebrin. If I could pick the land I was from, it would be Ebrin. We must help them."

"Me too Mel. And we will," Ed said.

Game to play: Campsite Set Up

Since many of the buildings are badly damaged, Mom, Dad, Ed, Mel, and Jax are helping set up a camp in Jalisp. There are two types of tents to be put up. The closed tents will be used for a temporary doctor's office and homes. The open tents will be used as dining areas and work areas. Help Ed and Mel set up the closed and open tents.

Materials needed:
- Game board and game cards. See Game Appendix.

Rules:
1. Draw a card.
2. Decide how many syllables the word has and what type of syllable each one is (open or closed).
3. Pick up a closed tent card for every closed syllable in the word. Pick up an open tent card for every open syllable in the word. Example: The word "he" has one syllable, which is open. Select one open tent card. The word "object" has two syllables, which are both closed. Select two closed tent cards.
4. Place the card or cards on the appropriate tent sites on the game board. If there are no more tent sites available for the type of tent the player has, discard the tent card into the discard pile.
5. It is now the next player's turn.
6. The first player to set up all the tents at their campsite wins the game.

Chapter 5

Additional required skills for student text:

Ability to read the sounds of "ex" as in extent vs. exam, and "al" as in also.

Barton Level: **Level 4 Lesson 5**.

Narrator (Parent or Tutor):

The next morning Mom, Dad, Ed, Mel, and Jax began making plans to catch up to R. L. Nox. They learned that after R. L. stole all the treasure in Jalisp, he headed to the rift, or gate, near the Market of Caltrez. He planned to use this gate to send his loot back to his world. Now they knew exactly where R. L. was headed. They also learned they were getting closer to him. He was only about 18 hours ahead. As they evaluated the situation, it became obvious that the group was going to have to split up. They needed to quicken their pace to catch up to R. L. Also, the people of Jalisp still needed their help.

Student text:

"Ed and Mel, your mother and I must help the Jalisp kin. Don't panic. Don't fret. We are sure your gifts will help you stop R. L. I expect your friend Jax will help with his gifts too," said Dad.

"Thanks, Dad. I am sure the Jalisp kin will be glad to have your help. Mel, Jax, and I will get R. L.," said Ed.

Mel added, "We will be back to Jalisp once we are done with R. L. We love you both so much!"

"Watch for pesky problems. We love you too," said Mom.

Ed, Mel, and Jax left Jalisp. In a bit Jax

said, "The rift R. L. will go to is this one on the map. I know a hidden path that will help us get there. It is taxing but quick. It will help us catch up. Do you trust me?"

"Jax, if you think we can do it, we trust that we can. We must catch up to R. L. I think we should try any tactic that will help us catch him," said Mel.

"Let's do it!" said Ed.

"O.K. We must trek up the gulch there on the left," Jax said as they began to walk off the path. "Watch your step. The land has dips and small pits that can twist your leg. You should pick up Ash so he doesn't fall into a pit."

Jax led them into the gulch. It wasn't long until the walls of the gulch did gulp up the small band. The small path led them to an open spot.

A sudden cliff did block their path, so they had to stop in the open spot. The lofty walls were so tall. Ed and Mel could not spy where to go next. It was a decent spot to rest.

Jax said, "Let's rest for a bit. Don't panic about the cliff. There is a rock that has a tip to find the spot where we can get past this cliff."

When they were done with their rest, Jax began to sniff. "I expect to find a rock which has an odd smell. A bad egg has this smell too. All I have to do is sniff for it. When I find it, we can access the hidden steps."

Ed and Mel began to sniff for the rock. Ash began to sniff. He didn't know why. He just did what Mel did. Mel almost got too dizzy to stand just as Ed had to rest.

Jax said, "You don't have to sniff that much. The rock stinks. You will smell it if you are by it." He did walk past a big clump of grass. "I think I smell it in this spot."

Ed and Mel ran to Jax. Ash began to run too, but he did stop when he could smell the rock. Mel did sniff again. It was a big sniff. Mel did gag. She was next to the odd stinky rock in the cliff.

Jax did study the spot next to Mel. He did push on two rocks in the cliff wall. A hidden step did unfold from the cliff with a pop and puff of dust. Then there was a string of pops. Dust did frolic on the wind and then did come to a rest.

Mel did gasp. A lavish sketch and cut-glass bits were on all the rock steps. The cut glass did catch the sun. It lit up all the steps which led up to the top of the cliff.

Jax said to Mel, "These steps are classic Ebrin. They are stunning and strong."

Ed said, "Let's get to the top of the cliff and focus on this problem with R. L.

Game to play: Step on Up

Ed, Mel, and Jax need to climb the steps on the cliff walls. Help them get from the bottom of the canyon to the top of the cliff walls.

Materials needed:
- One six-sided die.
- Game token for each player.
- Game board and game cards. See Game Appendix.

Rules:
1. Select a token for each player and place them on the "Start."
2. Roll the die.
3. Follow the directions on the game board chart based on the die roll.
4. First player to reach the "Finish" wins the game.
5. Reshuffle the cards if needed.

Chapter 6

Additional required skills for student text:

Ability to read Schwa in closed syllables.

Barton Level: **Level 4 Lesson 6**.

Narrator (Parent or Tutor):

Jax was right. The steps were classic Ebrin. They showed creativity. They showed out of the box thinking. They showed complex engineering, design skills, and 3-D reasoning. The cut glass was glowing in the sun. That made it much easier to see and climb the strong, sturdy steps. Without the glass, the steps would have blended in with the ground far below. Mel wondered if the glass art was meant to be a safety feature or not, but she was sure glad it was there. She was also impressed that Jax knew the land and shortcuts so well. The shortcut was a making a difference as they worked to catch up to R. L.

The climb took a lot of energy and concentration, but the trio reached the top of the cliff in a manner of minutes. The three hunters were getting closer to their prey. They were only a couple hours away from the Market of Caltrez.

Meanwhile, their prey was preparing his next move. R. L. Nox was indeed at the Market of Caltrez. He had used the rift near the market to take the plunder from Jalisp to his world where he had rented a warehouse. He arranged for his crew to process the plunder and prepare for more. His right-hand man, Fred, was setting up a store front for the more artsy items. The unusual expensive items would be sold on the black-market.

At the market in Ebrin, R. L. scanned through the merchants' booths. He couldn't help but dream of all the riches he would get for the various items he saw. The small rug hanging next to him was so well made and so beautiful, he knew he could sell it for $8,000. There was a stack of 100 or more small rugs in the booth. There were 20 to 30 large rugs. They were so beautiful that they could be sold for $40,000 to $50,000 each. The next booth had antique vases, which were brought to Ebrin generations ago. R. L. was sure they were Ming vases. Each vase could sell on the black-market for two to three million dollars.

R. L.'s greed made him giddy. He was enjoying making his "shopping" list, but he needed to focus on the gold. This gold would be worth tens of millions of dollars. He had left his small gold chunk with the designs back at his house. If he had it now, it would have been easier to find the merchant he needed. But that didn't matter now. He was in front of the merchant's booth. He stepped inside.

The merchant, Mr. Maddox, greeted R. L. with a large smile. He had a hard time expressing himself with many words, but he always made sure his customers knew he valued them through his expressions. He uttered a brief "Hello," and extended his hand to R. L.

R. L. firmly grabbed Mr. Maddox's hand and twisted it behind his back. Before the merchant knew what had happened, he was tasting the dirt on the floor. His surprised cry alerted his young daughter. She ran to her father but was met by R. L. instead.

After tying the two up and warning them to not make a sound, R. L. began to quiz Mr. Maddox.

Student text:

"If you love your child, you will help me," R. L. said. "I wish you no ill will. But she will have a lot of stress and upset if I don't get what I want."

Mr. Maddox did yelp, "No! I help! I help!"

R. L. got an evil grin and did ask, "Where does the gold come from?"

Mr. Maddox did panic. He began to huff and puff. He had to help this man to protect his child. But he didn't know what would happen if he told the secret of the gold. He told R. L., "You ask so much."

R. L. said, "I don't think so. I ask a very

modest thing. It is almost silly how small. You tell me one thing, and your child will still love. She will still walk. She will still be happy. Don't press your luck. Tell me now and hug your child again. Don't tell me, and you'll regret it."

Mr. Maddox began to cry a tiny bit. He had to defend his child. He had to tell the secret of the gold. He would trust that the Felkin of Ebrin would get why he had to tell the secret. He would trust they would not expel him from Ebrin.

Mr. Maddox began, "West. Past . . . past the dam. In the hill. There. The Felkin. The Felkin get the gold. Felkin tunnel . . . dig.

Felkin get it. Felkin protect it. You can't get it. Can't."

"Hmm," R. L. did think a bit. "O.K. That does help. Also, tell me how do I contend with the Felkin?"

This did shock Mr. Maddox. He said, "You don't. Don't cross Felkin. Don't."

R. L. did yell, "I do what I want! I will tell you what I will or won't do!" He did grab Mr. Maddox and said with an evil grunt, "Tell me."

"A cutlass. A cutlass with toxin. Toxin infect Felkin. Toxic pollen . . . alkon plant pollen. Stall #341. Alkon toxin at #341," Mr. Maddox did snivel.

R. L. did snap at his men. They hid Mr. Maddox and his child in a big, metal chest in the tent.

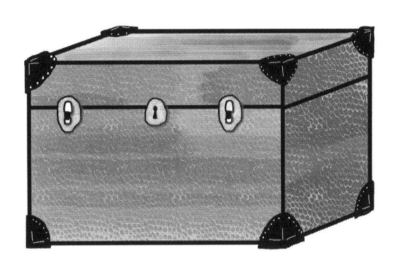

No one would find them for a bit. R. L. and his men began to walk to stall #341.

Game to play: Twisted Tic-Tac-Toe

Strategies can help us reach a goal. Sometimes there are things beyond our control that affect our strategies. R. L.'s first strategy for getting rich has been interrupted by Ed and Mel. He is adapting his strategy so he can work towards his goal of getting all the riches of Ebrin.

Play this tic-tac-toe game with a twist. The typical tic-tac-toe board makes choosing the center spot a good strategy. But what if a player's turn is skipped? What if the next move must be on a different tic-tac-toe board? Would strategies need to change? Depending on the word you draw, you may or may not be able to play your turn. You may need to come up with new or changing strategies to win at this game of tic-tac-toe.

Materials needed:

- Game board and game cards. See Game Appendix.
- Two different colors of counting chips or writing utensils.

Rules:

Version One – Read a Word with a Schwa to Play:

1. Player One: Draw a card. Read the word. Does the word have a schwa? If so, place your counting chip, "X," or "O" on tic-tac-toe board number <u>ONE</u>. If the word does not have a schwa, your turn is over. Do not place a chip or mark. It is now the next player's turn.

2. Player Two: Draw a card. Read the word. Does the word have a schwa? If so, place your counting chip, "X," or "O" on tic-tac-toe board number <u>TWO</u>. If the word does not have a schwa, your turn is over. Do not place a chip or mark. It is now the next player's turn.

3. Player One will play their next turn on board number <u>THREE</u>.

4. Player Two will play their next turn on board number <u>ONE</u>.

5. The turns will continue to rotate from board one to two to three. If a player is to play on a board, but they can't play due to reading a word without a schwa, the next player will make a move on that same board. When a board has been won by a player by placing 3 marks in a row, that board will be skipped for the rest of the game play.

6. The player who wins the most tic-tac-toe boards wins the game.

7. The game can be played with three or five tic-tac-toe boards.

<u>Version Two – Read a Word to Play</u>:

Play a game of traditional tic-tac-toe.

1. Player One: Draw a card. Read the word. Place your counting chip, "X," or "O" on the tic-tac-toe board. It is now the next player's turn.

2. Player Two: Draw a card. Read the word. Place your counting chip, "X," or "O" on the tic-tac-toe board. It is now the next player's turn.

3. The first player to get a full row of three wins the board.

4. Play all three games, one board at a time. The player who wins two out of the three boards (or three out of five boards) wins.

Chapter 7

Additional required skills for student text:

Ability to read two syllable words using the syllable division rule for three consonants between the vowels. (dividing vcccv) Ability to read compound words.

Barton Level: **Level 4 Lesson 7**.

Narrator (Parent or Tutor):

Jax's shortcut helped Ed, Mel, and him make up a lot of ground in catching R. L. They walked almost all night, only taking a few hours to sleep. Around noon they finally reached the east side of the Market of Caltrez. Little did they know how close they were to R. L. Nox.

Jax knew most of the merchants at the market. Jax approached the nearest merchant, who happened to be a dear friend.

"Hi there, Orin!" Jax said. "Have you seen a stranger asking a lot of questions? He would have some other strangers with him."

"Hello, Jax! Good to see you!" Orin replied. "I haven't seen anyone like that yet today. I do know you and your friends look like hungry travelers. My delicious food will help sustain you on your search. Please, have some food." "What do you think?"

Ed's stomach grumbled. Mel realized how hungry she was, and Ash whimpered for some food. So they quickly ordered a meal. Orin wouldn't allow them to pay. They thanked him, ate, and continued their search.

They ran into several merchants who had seen R. L. The merchants couldn't say where he had gone, though. They did tell Ed, Mel, and Jax that he had been there earlier that morning. One merchant last saw him leaving the gold merchant's tent. Ed, Mel, and Jax hurried to the gold merchant's tent.

"That's odd," Jax remarked as they entered the vacant tent. "There is no one here. I know Mr. Maddox. He would not leave his tent unstaffed. He cares too much about his customers to not have someone greet them. R. L. did something." They looked around some more and decided to go to the next merchant to see if he knew where Mr. Maddox was. As they were leaving, there was a quiet thump which came from the chest in the corner. The trio turned around and opened the chest.

There they found Mr. Maddox and his daughter tied and gagged. They quickly freed them. Ash sat next to Mr. Maddox's daughter and licked her face. Jax asked about R. L.

Student text:

   "Jax! This is bad. Bad!" said Mr. Maddox. "That bad man. He went to the Felkin. The Felkin! He went to rob them! I protect my child. I told. I had to. Didn't want to. No. Felkin will be in distress. Alkon distress. He will kill Felkin!"

   Jax felt sick. This problem was brutal. If R. L. did rob all the gold, that was one thing. They could put up with that because they would still go on with what they had left. If R. L. did kill the Felkin, Ebrin could not last. It would be the end of Ebrin. "Ed and Mel," Jax said. "If R. L. does kill the Felkin, Ebrin will not last. The Felkin dig the gold from the bottom of the tunnels in the hills. They also help adjust vents in the rock. This does stop the stress put on the rock by gas. The gas will push and compress the rocks if they do not vent the gas. The rocks will begin to twist and grind. It will send hundreds of jolts across the land. Only the Felkin can control the vents. It will be a risk to even walk in Ebrin."

"Who are the Felkin? How can we help them?" Mel did ask.

"The Felkin are what you would call a dragon," Jax said. Ed and Mel both did gasp.

"You said dragon? As in big dino? With

fangs? And that can puff so hot it would fry things? Dragons exist?" Ed did ask. Ed would panic about a small mammal that could have fangs. He ran from Ash when he met him. If Ash was a level one risk, a dragon would be a level ten.

Jax said, "Yes, a Felkin is a dragon. It won't fry a friend that does help them. It will try to fry you if you combat it. But they are still at risk when R. L. does get there. Alkon is a toxin that can kill them. If they are cut with a cutlass that has the toxin, it will be bad."

"Well then," said Mel, "we will help the Felkin. It will be quick to catch up to R. L.

now."

Ed did gulp and said, "Let's do it. I trust the Felkin won't fry me. Jax, I have a plan. Mr. Maddox, you get some help from the public. We will get a mob to protect the Felkin. Also, can you find a cutlass stash to equip the mob? If there is a balm, a drug, to stop the toxin, we will have to get that too."

"Yes, yes! A mob and a cutlass stash. Balm with saffron. A doc too. I will get Doc. Doc can come. We protect the Felkin!" Mr. Maddox ran off to do his tasks. Jax left behind him.

"Ed," Mel said, "don't fret about the Felkin. It's R. L. we must stop. We must focus on the skills we have to do this. You have a skill to rally this mob. This plan will be a success if we act as one. To act as one, we must have someone to command the mob. I trust you can do it."

"Thanks Mel," Ed said. "We will want your wisdom for this job. It will help in the conflict. Help me get a checklist and finish the plan."

Game to play: Gather and Go

Ed, Mel, Jax, and Mr. Maddox are gathering resources to save the Felkin. Use your reading skills to gather the resources from around the board before your opponent.

Materials needed:
- Game board and game cards. See Game Appendix.
- Two six-sided dice.
- Game tokens.

Rules:
1. Draw a card and read the word.
2. Roll the dice and move the token that number of spaces along one of the paths towards a resource. If a player reaches a resource circle, collect the resource card for that resource and the turn is over.
3. On a player's next turn after collecting a resource card, the player will make their way back to the "Start/End" circle before choosing a different path to a different resource. They do not have to stop on the "Start/End."
4. The player who has collected all four resource cards and returns to the "Start/End" first wins the game.

Chapter 8

Narrator (Parent or Tutor):

It wasn't long before Jax and Mr. Maddox returned with a large crowd. The merchants were ready to protect the Felkin and Ebrin. Ed shared the plan with them and organized them into smaller groups. Jax helped him select leaders for each of the groups. Ed met with them before they all headed west.

As they traveled, Mel learned as much as she could about Felkin first aid from the doctor. She learned how to use the balm and drugs to give the dragons a fighting chance against the toxin. It was a lot of information, but her passion for helping animals gave her the focus she needed to learn and remember all that Doc said. Her lessons about chemistry from her last science class helped her make sense of his directions as well.

Ed knew they had to pick up the pace and yet still be ready for battle instead of a nap when they reached R. L. and the Felkin. He set a good pace and watched to see how the mob was keeping up. He was pleased to see that they were keeping up easily.

Soon Ed reached the top of a ridge. In the valley below a fierce battle raged. There was R. L. Nox.

He was battling four large dragons with his men. He had set up several mobile shelters, which gave his men cover from the dragons' fire. When the dragons focused on attacking one or two of the shelters, men ran out from the others, slashing at the dragons' legs. Then they ducked back to the shelter while another group charged the dragons' legs.

Jax stood by Ed. "They don't have to kill the dragons with the cutlasses," he said. "They only have to cut the dragons with the poisoned blades. The dragons' scales will stop most of the blows, but as they move, small gaps are vulnerable to being cut."

Ed took a deep breath and gave Jax a resolved look.

Student text:

"Let's do this," Ed said. He held his cutlass up to the sky and led the mob with a shrill cry. The mob did match the cry and ran to the bottom of the hill to combat.

R. L. did whip about to look at the racket on the hill. He was upset. These children were pests! This would be their end if he could help it. R. L. did yell at his men to split up. "Cut the dragons and stop that mob!"

Some of Nox's men left the dragons to confront all the people. The clash of metal rang through the cry of the mob.

Ed did slam into a man. The man fell.

On the right a man swung at Ed. He had to duck and jump back. His friends did help push R. L.'s men back. Ed got hit on the chin. It began to throb, but he kept going.

Mel did witness a dragon dragging a man through the grass. He was in distress. She did help Jax push some men back. A hot blast went past Jax and Mel as a dragon did cover their path to R. L.

Mr. Maddox fell next to Ed. Ed did defend the spot where Mr. Maddox fell until he got up. They too did push past the men to get to R. L.

R. L. did slam his fists on a camel's rump. "Blast these kids! Blast the Ebrin people! Why do they have to mess up my plans? You!" he did yell. "Go to the left flank and cut them into bits!"

Ed's plan was going well. The Ebrin people did defend the left flank. They did push R. L.'s men back. The people and the dragons upset the strongholds bit by bit.

R. L. did know he had lost this conflict. He was so mad but would not quit. He was quick to think of a plan to get what he had come for. He could put up with a small holdup in his plans. He did yell to his men to fall back. They would run for now. He would be back.

"Mel!" Ed did yell. "R. L. is on the run.

We must catch him!"

"Ed," Mel said. "I don't think we can hunt him now. Some of the people are cut. The dragons all have cuts. We have to focus on the toxin. It will kill the dragons. That is our big problem now."

Ed did watch R. L. Nox run off into the sunset. It was brutal to watch him go, but Ed was sure that they would cross paths again. "I wish I could be in two spots at once," he said. Then he did walk back to the dragons.

Game to play: The Battle

Materials needed:

- Game board and game cards. See Game Appendix.
- Four different colored counting chips or markers. Six of color number one. Six of color number two. Two of color number three and eighteen of color number four.

Game board setup:

Player One puts six markers (one color) in spaces 13-24. Player Two puts six markers (one color) in spaces 13-24. Place two dragon markers (one color) in spots 9 and 10. Put Nox's army (eighteen markers of one color) in all the blank spots.

Rules:

1. Draw a card.
2. Read the word in bold font.
3. Follow the move directions on the card: The first move is by Nox's army. Move any Nox soldier marker that is not on a numbered space to the numbered space on the card. If there are no Nox soldier markers left on an unnumbered space, you can start moving soldiers from any of the other numbered spots. If a player or dragon is on the space where a soldier lands, the player or dragon's chip is removed from the board.
4. If there is a dragon move listed, it will be the second move made. The dragon can move any direction, and change directions. It will take out every Nox soldier it touches. A dragon that can move three spaces could remove up to three soldier markers from the board.

5. The last move on the card is for the player's own marker. The player can only move in one direction at a time and cannot move diagonally. The player can only remove a soldier if they land on a space with a soldier. If they pass over a soldier, that soldier remains on the board. If a player chooses to move fewer spaces in order to land on a space with a soldier, they may do so.

6. Reshuffle and read through the cards again if needed.

7. Battle until the players and dragons win by removing all of Nox's soldiers, or until the soldiers win by removing all the players and dragons. This is a player versus environment game, not a player versus player game. If players want to compete against each other, they can keep track of how many soldiers they remove from the board. The player who removes the most soldiers wins the game.

Chapter 9

Additional required skills for student text:

Ability to apply syllable division rules to words that have more than two syllables.

Barton Level: **Level 4 Lesson 9**.

The word "ugh" is used with the silent "h."

Narrator (Parent or Tutor):

Ed walked around the battlefield to check on the wounded. Just as Mel had said, all the dragons had a cut of some sort. The poison was starting to affect the battle-weary dragons. The smallest dragon collapsed. Mel, the doctor, Mr. Maddox, and several others were busy preparing the balm and drugs they had brought from the market.

Ed found Jax with a few of the Ebrinite merchants. He had a large gash on his arm. Several of the merchants were wandering around. A few were crying softly. Some sat quietly on the grass.

Ed knew he wasn't finished leading. He took a deep breath and began to address the crowd.

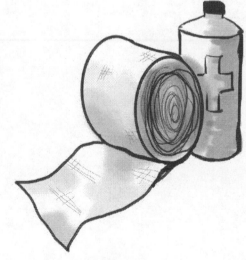

Student text:

   "People of Ebrin. We did stop the momentum of R. L. to kill the Felkin. We did push back and defend Ebrin from this evil. We must hang on and help the Felkin combat the toxin. Ebrin is dependent on what we do now." Some people did nod and others did clap.

   Ed went on, "The people who could do with some help, lift a flag or hand. The people who are well must help these people with cuts. Patch them up and get them something to drink. Also, I ask that two people look for anything strange on the crest of the hill. Ten people will set up camp so others can rest. Jax will direct the camp set up there by the hill. Seven people should help Mel and the doc with the dragons. Mel, do you have anything to add?"

"Thanks, Ed. Yes, I want cloth and a bunch of the wet stuff from the pond. Someone must get the two baby dragons from the den and bring them to their mother. We will also get them something to munch. We will set up shifts to swish the cuts with meds and wet stuff. The balm will help combat the toxin," Mel did finish.

The people got busy with their tasks. Ed sat on a big rock to think things through. "I wish R. L. didn't find an exit. I'm happy he left the dragons, but I did want to stop R. L. We almost had him. Ugh! I can't stop thinking about it even if my chin is throbbing. I guess I should patch my chin up." Ed got up and met up with Jax.

"Jax, did you patch up your gash?" Ed did ask.

"Yep. You should have doc look at that chin." Jax said.

"That is my present task." Ed said. "How is the camp getting on?"

"Well. The big jobs are almost done. Let's find the doc for you." Jax said.

"Sure. Then I will study my lessons to

lessen this spell. If I can't hunt R. L. at the moment, I can still combat the spell. Its potency will diminish if I study," said Ed.

With his chin on the mend, Ed did study for a bit. Then he did watch a baby dragon as it snuck up on Mel and did push her hand. Mel did jump. Then she did grin. The dragon did rest on her leg. Ed went to help Mel. He began to pat the dragon. It did roll up into a ball next to him. He wasn't sure, but the dragon did act happy.

Mel had a big grin. She did know that Ed had to be strong and bold to help her with the dragon. Not long ago, he ran from Ash. He would run from any living thing that wasn't human. Now, he was petting a dragon.

As dusk began to set, the person on duty to look after the camp began to yell, "There is a man on the path to the camp!" Ed, Mel, and Jax ran to the path. There was a skinny man from the shops. "I know him," Jax said. "Hi, Twigs. What's up?" Jax said.

"Hello there, Jax," said Twigs. "I was on a trek in the hills. I did pass a band of men. Many of them had cuts. Now I know where they got them. Did something big happen?"

They told Twigs all of it. He said, "Well,

I can tell you where they've set up their camp. I don't think they'll travel very fast. I'll tell you all I know about the camp."

Twigs told them where R. L.'s camp was and how big it was, including how many men were there. Then Ed did ask Mel, "If we get a band to go to R. L.'s camp, will the dragons be O.K. at this camp?"

Mel said, "Yes, with the balm and some love, they are on the mend. They are dependent on the balm, but it is helping. With the doc and Mr. Maddox, they should be O.K."

"Let's go apprehend R. L. Nox," Ed did grin.

Game to play: Picking Up the Pieces

After the battle Ed, Mel, Jax, and the Ebrinites set up camp and tended to the wounded. As Ed rested and studied, he reflected on how the smaller tasks people were completing actually completed the larger task of setting up the camp. He noticed how multiple syllable words worked the same way. It was reading the smaller syllables that helped him read the longer multisyllable words. If he tried to skip reading the smaller syllables, it was harder to read the long words. He was reading the longer word by reading the smaller syllables, just like the camp was coming together because people were completing smaller jobs. Build the words on your game card syllable by syllable. The first player to build all the words on their game card wins.

Materials needed:
- Game board and game cards. See Game Appendix.

Rules:
1. Pick one of the three pages of game boards to play. On that page, select which player will play on game board #1 and board #2. Have the reference sheet available if needed.
2. <u>Round One</u>:
    a. Player One: Draw a card from the draw pile. If the syllable exists in a word on Player One's board, put the card down in the correct space. If the syllable exists on Player Two's board, discard the card into discard pile number one. If the syllable isn't in a word on either player's board, discard the card into discard pile number two. It is now Player Two's turn.

b. Keep playing until all the cards from the draw pile have been read and placed on a board or discarded into one of the discard piles.

3. <u>Round Two</u>:

   a. Turn discard pile number one into the new draw pile and continue play.

   b. If you need to discard a card, put it on the bottom of the draw pile.

   c. Keep playing until a player fills up all the boxes on their game board. The first player who fills all the spaces on their game board wins the game.

   d. If the cards were discarded incorrectly during the first round, play until all the cards from discard pile one have been used. The player with the most spaces filled on their board wins the game.

Chapter 10

Additional required skills for student text:

Ability to recognize when open-a turns to schwa.

Barton Level: **Level 4 Lesson 10**.

Note: The words "word" and "words" are used in this chapter. They are underlined. They are used out of sequence from the Barton Reading & Spelling System scope and sequence.

Narrator (Parent or Tutor):

Ed was hopeful the end of the hunt was near. He organized the Ebrinites who were still strong enough to go to R. L.'s camp. Doc and Mr. Maddox would stay with a small group who would care for the dragons and the injured.

Twigs gave Ed and Jax all the details of R. L.'s camp location and layout. Twigs remembered quite a bit about the camp. It was helpful information. Ed was sure it would allow the group to sneak up and surprise R. L. Hopefully they could catch him without much of a fight, but they were ready to do what was needed to stop R. L. Twigs was too worn out from his long journey to join the fight. He promised he would help take care of the wounded at camp.

The plan was coming together. After they found the camp, they would stay hidden while Jax found the tent R. L. was sleeping in. After he found R. L., Jax would signal the group. They would rush in and capture R. L. before he knew what was going on. After a few hours of sleep and a few of travel, they would finally have R. L. Ed and Mel could hardly wait.

Ed, Mel, and Jax rose from their rest just after midnight and said their goodbyes. Ash whimpered as Mel hugged him goodbye. He had to stay with Mr. Maddox. Mel couldn't let the energetic fluff ball come with her. His energy didn't fit well with their surprise attack plan. Soon everyone was ready to go.

The journey went smoothly as they quietly marched down the moonlit trail. As they neared R. L.'s camp, they were more cautious. They didn't want to alert any scouts or those in the camp. Finally, they were in position.

Student Text:

"Ed, my instinct is that this is going to be bad," Jax said.

"Is there anything that is off about the camp?" Ed did ask.

"No. The intel is exact. The camp is there. I don't spot anything odd," Jax said.

"Do we have any basis to call off the attack?" Mel did ask.

"No, not that I can think of," said Jax. "It is just something in my gut."

"I think we should stick to the plan," Mel said. "We have to stop R. L. and this is our shot. I think it is the stress. Stress can mess with your instinct. We can't let R. L.

go now."

They couldn't find any basis to call off the attack. So Jax left to do his recon. Ed, Mel, and the rest did look for the signal.

"Ed, listen. Did you catch that? That was a cry from across the camp," said Mel. "There it is again."

"Listen up. Something is happening. Look for R. L.'s men," Ed said.

One moment there was nothing. The next moment, they all did spot Jax running as fast as he could from the camp. He was yelling, "It's a trap! It's a trap! Abandon the plan!" Behind him were many big, big insects. The baby ones had the bulk of big biceps. The adult ones were as big as Jax's full leg. The insects had body segments and abundant legs. Ed did want to run back to the Felkin. These insects did want him for lunch. But Ed did not abandon Mel, Jax, and the gang. He had to protect his friends and stop R. L.

"The bugs in Alaska don't look so big now," Mel did gulp. She held her cutlass up.

Jax did jump into the mob of friends. He only had a moment to tell the others how to combat the insects. He did gulp, "Cut them in two with a cutlass. If there is one segment link, you have to cut in front of the segment link. If it won't cut, then you have to cut it behind the link. If there are two links, cut in the mid spot. If there are two plus segment links, try to cut it behind the one in front. That will kill them. You can grab an antenna to help hold them."

Mel did ask, "What!? That was too quick! How do we cut them again?"

"If you can cut a <u>word</u> into chunks, you can cut an insect to kill it. Think of the links as consonants. You can do the dividing with your cutlass!" Jax did yell.

To combat the spell, Ed and Mel did study dividing <u>words</u>. They did know what to do. It was a lucky thing, because they were within the grasp of the insects.

A hefty insect did slam into Ed. Mel cut it in front of its one segment link as she did think of how to push one consonant to the end chunk in a <u>word</u>. It went limp and fell in the mud. At that moment, two other insects did grab onto Mel. Jax and Ed did dispatch these so she could run from their grasp.

The combat with the insects was wild. The frenzy was so robust, it had the band fretful that they wouldn't get through it.

As Ed, Mel, and Jax were busy with the insects, R. L. was busy back at the shops. With the dragons and his trap, most of the people were not at the shops. The people who were still there were not a problem for his men.

R. L. did ransack the shops. He did pack up the rugs, the Ming pots, and all the things on his list. He sent them to Fred, who was expecting the products back in his land.

R. L. was mad at Ed and Mel, so he did grin as he did reflect on the trap he set with the lethal insects. He didn't want to have to contend with them again.

Game to play: Insect War

Ed and Mel never thought that all their practice dividing words into syllables would be put into use in battle. But when you don't have time to think, you do what you have practiced. Ed and Mel were glad they had spent time practicing their syllable division over and over. All that practice was now helping to save their lives. Join the battle in a game of Insect War.

Materials needed:
- Game cards. See Game Appendix.

Rules:
1. Deal all the cards to the two players. Do not look at the cards.
2. Each player will play the top card from their pile by putting it down on the table face up.
3. If both cards are swords, each player will read the word on their cards and then place another card.
   If both cards are insects, each player will read each syllable separately before reading the word. Both players will place another card.
   If one player plays a sword card and the other plays an insect card, the player who played the sword card wins all the cards on the table if they read the word on the card correctly. If they don't read the word correctly, the player who played the insect card has a chance to win all the cards on the table by reading their word correctly.
4. Play for a set amount of time or until a player has won all the cards. The person who has the most cards, or all the cards, wins the game.

Chapter 11

Additional required skills for student text:

When to read open-i or open-e with their short vowel sounds. For those not using Barton, this is a variation of schwa. Barton users can refer to the notes on the Lesson 11 Overview page in their Barton manual.

Barton Level: **Level 4 Lesson 11**.

Narrator (Parent or Tutor):

The insects were relentless in their attack. The group fought bravely, but they kept losing ground. The insects weren't protecting the camp. Their goal was to destroy Ed, Mel, and the Ebrinites. Finally, Ed was able to lead the Ebrinite crew in a retreat away from the insects. They were fortunate to escape R. L.'s trap with their lives. They were weary, injured, and defeated. Ed knew that he would have nightmares of the centipede-like giant insects. He would have nightmares about how he failed the Ebrinites. He worried about the others. They escaped R. L.'s trap, but they needed to recover from the battle. They were closer to the market than the Felkin camp, so Ed led the group towards the market.

After a bit, Ed stopped the group for a rest. A small creek nearby provided fresh water to the weary group. After an hour's rest, they would walk the last leg to the market. Jax was checking on Mel's injuries, when an alert was raised. Two people were running from the direction of the market. Everyone grabbed their weapons and prepared for another attack. As the people got closer, an Ebrinite father let out a cry, dropped his weapon, and ran to his children, who were approaching. They were scared and crying. Seeing their father with the battered group made them cry even harder. He embraced them and asked them what was wrong.

Student text:

"That bad man was at the shops," the children did cry. "He did rob the shops. They are empty. He has it all, and now he has left. Are you O.K., father?"

"Yes, I will be O. K. You will be O. K. too. I will protect you," the father said. He then did look up at Ed with a look of distress.

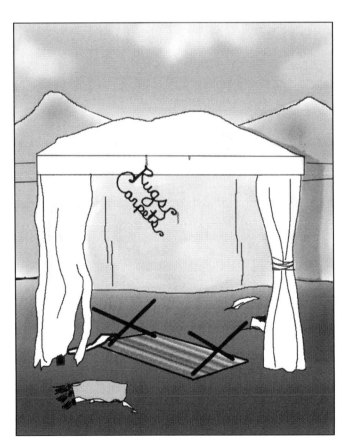

The people were all upset. They got up and went as fast as they could to the shops.

Ed was in shock. His job was to stop R. L. He was to help these people. His plan fell flat, did flop, and did crash. Ed felt R. L. would win now.

Mel did walk up to Ed and said, "This is my slip-up. If I did listen to Jax and his instinct, we would not have kept to the plan. We would have left it. Jax knew something was strange at the camp. I bet you would have had us get to the rift. We would have been there to catch R. L. and his men. I did mess up, and the insects did almost kill us."

"Mel," Ed did respond, "It is my mess up too. I did want to get R. L. so much that

I was too confident. When Jax was hesitant, well, I didn't listen."

"You two!" Jax did call out. "Listen up! This criminal is a difficult enemy! I could have not stuck to the plan, but I did. The camp did look O.K., and I did trust Twigs. He set us up. We couldn't know it was a trap."

"If you were not here, do you think an innocent R. L. would be a benefit to the Ebrin people? No! He would still rob us and mess up Jalisp, the Felkin, and the shops. It is evident that R. L. is the problem. You are the only ones who can help us stop him. The people of Ebrin stand by you.

Let's get to the shops and go from there."

Ed, Mel, and Jax went to the shops. They were in shreds, just as R. L. had left Jalisp. The people went back to what was left of their shops. Jax said, "Look, the people are O.K. If each citizen had been at their shop when R. L. held up them up, it would have been bad. R. L. did grab all the stuff, but he didn't mess with the people."

"Let's be practical. I know that our recent hunt has been a loss, but we are still on the hunt. R. L. can't do what he wants. You are still helping the people."

"Yes, Jax. I know," Mel said. "It is just so sad to have R. L. inflict agony on others.

I can't stand it."

"I know, Mel. We will get him. We will get him," Jax said.

A father, mother and son did dish up some lunch for Ed, Mel, and Jax. Then they went to dish up lunch for the next bunch. Some other people began to pick up trash.

"I am going to rest for a moment, then I will help pick up some of this mess," said Mel.

Jax said, "The people are O. K. They will mend. We should rest too, Ed. We have to mend a bit as well."

Game to play: Rebuild

Help rebuild the Market of Caltrez by setting up the market stalls. Build a market stall by drawing the walls to the stall.

Materials needed:
- Game board and game cards. See Game Appendix.

Rules:
1. Player One picks a card, reads the word, and makes a line between two dots.
2. If Player One finishes a stall (closes off a box) by drawing the fourth side, they will put their initials in the finished stall and take another turn. If the line they draw does not finish a stall, their turn is over. It is now Player Two's turn.
3. Play continues until a set amount of time is up or all the stalls have been built (all the boxes have been drawn).
4. The player who has their initials on the most market stalls wins the game.

Chapter 12

Additional required skills for student text:

Vowel teams ay and ee. "Y" at the end of multiple syllable words read as the long I sound.

Barton Level: **Level 4 Lesson 12**.

Note: Sentinel(s): a watchman (watchmen) or guard (guards)

Narrator (Parent or Tutor):

As the Ebrinites recovered, R. L. took some time sorting his stolen goods. His trap worked wonderfully as a distraction while he cleaned out the market. He hoped it also put an end to the trouble the Davis twins were causing him. Time would tell. As he checked items off his wish list, R. L. thought about the dragons and gold. He needed to come up with a plan to go back and collect his gold. He didn't have any more of the alkon toxin needed to weaken and kill the dragons. He had to find another way.

R. L.'s man, Fred, delivered his coffee. He commented, "The guys have been talking about those dragons. I bet they were something else. I can't believe you got to see a real dragon. It figures I was stuck back at this warehouse. I would have given anything to see a real breathing dragon."

R. L. put his coffee down and slowly said, "Really. That is very interesting. So you think you would pay to see them if I could arrange it?"

"Oh, yeah!" Fred responded. "As long as I wasn't in the line of fire, I would pay to see them. I bet my cousin in Russia would travel to see it. He is a dragon freak. Oh, and Benny's friend, his family has a thing about dragons. Arthur's son loves dinosaurs and has that book about training a dragon or something. I'm sure he would like to see a dragon."

"That is all," R. L. dismissed Fred.

A new plan began to form in R. L.'s brain. Maybe he was selling himself short by focusing on the gold. If he could bring a small dragon or two back to his world, everyone would want to see them. That meant everyone would pay admission. There would be no videos or pictures allowed except for the ones he sold. Then there was the merchandise line he could launch. He started to run some numbers as an evil grin returned to his face. This plan was sounding better and better. R. L. decided he would slip into Ebrin with a few tools while the dragons were still feeling the effects of the alkon toxin.

"Fred!" R. L. shouted. "I've got a new job for you. I want you to take some of our profits and go buy that circus outfit down the road. Do what needs to be done to make that happen. Make sure it has an enclosure that would hold a dragon. I'm going back to Ebrin. I'm going to go get myself a dragon."

"Oh yeah! Right away, Boss!" Fred exclaimed.

"I'm going to see a real dragon!" Fred exclaimed to himself as he turned to get started on his new task.

Student text:

At the Felkin camp, Mr. Maddox and Doc did check on the dragons. They were resting. The baby dragons did snug up to their mother. The dragons were on the mend, but they were still at risk. In a day to two days, they would know if the dragons would be okay.

Mr. Maddox did spray meds onto a cut on the big dragon. He was sad for the Felkin. He was sad about the shops.

Ed had sent three sentinels to notify the Felkin camp about the shops. Also, they were to look for any attack on the camp. The sentinels told the camp how Twigs did betray them.

Twigs had left camp once Ed, Mel, and Jax left for R. L.'s camp. The sentinels would catch him if they did find him.

Mr. Maddox did finish with the dragon meds. He did help Doc put the baby dragons into a paddock. That would let their mother get some rest. It was the end of the day. All was still and silent at camp. Mr. Maddox went to his tent to rest.

To his dismay, it was still black when Mr. Maddox got up. It was odd for him to get up when it was still black. Was it because he had to pee? No. He felt he should check on the dragons. So, he put on his pants and went to see the dragons.

When he got to the dragons, he could see something was off. Thick string held them so that they would stay in one spot. Mr. Maddox ran to get Doc. He wasn't very silent, and some others got up as well. It wasn't long until the dragons were free, but the baby dragons were gone.

Doc did yell, "Where did you put the two baby dragons?"

"In the paddock. I did help you," Mr. Maddox did reply.

"Did they run away?" a lady did ask.

"No. Look. The lock is cut. Someone did this," Doc said. "Did the sentinels see anything?"

The top sentinel did reply, "No, but Ray was the sentinel by the dragons, and he is gone too. Let's check the camp. Get the lamps. We must all look for the baby dragons and Ray. Don't delay!"

A quick check of the camp did result in finding Ray. He had a big bump on his noggin. His hands and legs were held by string, the kind that had held the dragons. He had been put behind a tent. No one did find the baby dragons.

When Ray was with it again, he said, "One second I was okay. The next second, a big man was in front of me with a big bat. He had an excellent swing because I don't know anything past that."

"Was it one of R. L.'s men?" the sentinel did ask.

"It had to be. He had that odd clothing from Ed and Mel's land," Ray did reply. "Where is Bree? She did see the man too."

"I don't see Bree anywhere," said Doc. "R. L. must have her too."

The sentinel sent a man to notify Ed in Caltrez. It was critical for Ed, Mel, and Jax to get back to the Felkin camp.

Game to play: BAM!

Ray is recovering from the dangerous hit he took from R. L.'s man. It is important to avoid being hit by a bat, or there are consequences. Play a game of BAM! and avoid drawing the BAM! card.

Materials needed:
- Game cards. See Game Appendix.

Rules:
1. Shuffle the cards and place them in a draw pile.
2. Player One draws a card, reads it and keeps the card. It is Player Two's turn. If a BAM! card is drawn, the player must put all his cards into the discard pile.
3. Keep playing until the draw pile is empty or time runs out. The player who has the most cards wins the game.

Chapter 13

Additional required skills for student text:

Vowel teams ow, oe, ew, ue.

Barton Level: **Level 4 Lesson 13**.

The word "ugh" is used with the silent "h."

Narrator (Parent or Tutor):

The messenger entered the Market of Caltrez. It was already looking better than when he had seen it a few days ago. The Ebrinite people were resilient and hard working. The sight would have lifted his spirits if it wasn't for the bad news he had to deliver. He found Ed and Mel. Jax was helping them study at Mr. Maddox's shop. He took a deep breath and told them about the missing baby dragons.

Ed, Mel, and Jax didn't hesitate. They grabbed a few items and left Caltrez as soon they heard the news. They took some more balm for the dragons and a few other supplies for the Felkin camp. Ed also decided to send word to his parents in Jalisp. He was hoping they could come to the Felkin camp. It seemed that every time they caught up to R. L., he slipped away or had a trick up his sleeve. The game was getting old. Something was going to have to change, but he didn't know what it was. Mel and Jax were out of ideas as well. Talking to his parents might help them figure it out.

As they entered the Felkin camp, Mr. Maddox ran up to Ed and Mel. Ash bounced past Mr. Maddox and jumped into Mel's arms. Mel buried her face into Ash's soft fur. He nuzzled into her neck. She had missed the little fur ball.

Student text:

"So sad. The baby dragons. Gone. Bree too," lamented Mr. Maddox.

"I don't get what R. L. wants with the dragons," Ed said. "Is there a ransom, um, you know . . . a ransom . . . ugh, a ransom memo?"

"No. Just gone," said Mr. Maddox.

Mel felt her body sway a bit. She put Ash on the grass and sat next to him. "Ed, I must sit for a few. I must be dizzy. I don't know why."

Jax put his hand up for Mel to grab. "It is not just you, Mel," Jax said. "The land is a bit askew. Look at the camp."

All the people did stop in their tracks as the land did shift a tiny bit. It didn't last long, but the people did know this was not the last jolt for the land. If the Felkin didn't get back to the tunnels to tend the vents, the shocks would expand in frequency and intensity.

"R. L. isn't our only enemy. The clock is not our friend," Ed said.

"The Felkin have to get back to tend the vents. If there is a delay, the shocks will demolish Ebrin," Jax did agree. "Also, even if the Felkin get well and rescue the land, we will have this problem again when it is the baby Felkin's responsibility to tend the vents."

Ed did reply, "Let us check on the Felkin and see to it that they can go back to the tunnels. We will have to come up with a plan for the rest."

They went to see Doc and the dragons. Three of the them were almost well. They were slow, but they could walk through the camp. The small one was still not well. Doc did mix up the new balm and put it on its cuts. It was evident that she was in distress.

A small jolt again hit the land. Doc said, "These three Felkin will get back to the vents at the next sunup. Don't fret about that."

"That's excellent," said Jax.

"Well, we still have a problem," said Doc. "The small Felkin is not well. She may not last until sunup."

Mel went to sit with the small Felkin and put her hand on its neck. "Stay with us," she wept.

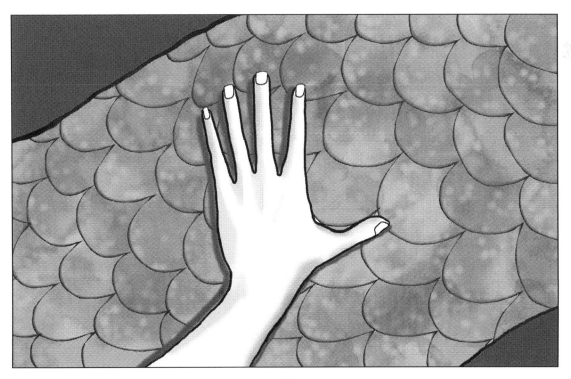

Game to play: Rhyming Road

Ed and Mel didn't hesitate to go back to the Felkin camp when they heard the news. It felt like they were getting farther away from their goal of catching R. L., but sometimes there are things that deserve attention before moving on. Each step of the journey is meaningful, even if it feels like it is not heading the right direction.

Materials needed:

- Game board and game cards. See Game Appendix.

Rules:

1. Player One, roll the dice and move that number of spaces on the board.
2. Draw a card and read the word, or follow the directions on the card.
3. If the card has a word to read and it rhymes** with the word on the space where Player One's token landed, move ahead two extra spaces.
4. Put the card in the discard pile. It is now Player Two's turn.
5. Reshuffle the game cards if needed.
6. The player who reaches the end first wins.

**There are some variations in types of rhymes especially where there is more than one syllable. Play with the last syllable rhyming (End rhyme[1]). Since the words in this game all end in vowel sounds, there will be a lot of end rhymes. Banjo and willow and toe all rhyme.

[1] (Rhyme. (n.d.). Retrieved March 28, 2020, from https://www.poetryfoundation.org/learn/glossary-terms/rhyme)

Chapter 14

Additional required skills for student text:

Vowel teams ai, oa.

Barton Level: **Level 4 Lesson 14**.

Narrator (Parent or Tutor):

Meanwhile, R. L. Nox was giddy. Things were looking up. First, he hadn't seen anything of the Davis family in days. Second, his warehouse was full. Third, money was starting to roll in. People were amazed at the quality of the products he was selling, and word was spreading fast. And last, he was the proud owner of a circus with an attraction so wonderful, the whole world would soon be wanting to give him lots of money to see it. Yes, it was a good day.

At noon he was going to see how Bree and the circus master were doing with the dragons' accommodations. Bree hadn't wanted to help, but it didn't take much to convince her that the dragons would die without her care. R. L. felt fortunate that she was comforting the babies when he came to steal them. It wasn't hard to take her with the dragons.

Maybe operating on the fly had its advantages. He had always been such a planner. If things didn't fit the plan, he wouldn't try them. But Ed and Mel forced him to change his plans and think on his feet. The last few weeks had been such a pain. R. L. was out of his comfort zone, but after all that trouble, he was in a better spot than he had first planned. Maybe the trouble Ed and Mel had caused him had helped him grow and become a better villain. He leaned back in his chair and laughed.

Student text:

Back at camp, Ed and Mel sat with their mom and dad. They had left Jalisp and got to the Felkin camp as fast as they could.

"Don't cry, Mel," Mom said, "The dragon may still pull through. You both have done so much. The other three dragons are well and will continue to tend the gas vents deep in the hills. You did rescue and help Ebrin. Keep that in mind."

Ed said, "But all that we have done isn't . . . it isn't . . . AHHH! This stupid spell! I did fail! Yes, the three dragons are well, but Ebrin was almost devastated! The one dragon is still not well."

"The baby dragons are lost. Bree is lost. R. L. did rob Jalisp and the shops at Caltrez. People are in pain. Mel and Jax were almost toast when the big insects did approach them."

"My goal is to stop R. L., and he is still free. I should just quit. It would be best if I quit. I don't belong. I'm not a help. Even with my gifts I'm rubbish!"

Dad held Ed in a strong hug. Mel did cry in Mom's lap. Then the ill dragon began to bellow. It did look at Ed and Mel and did bellow again.

Jax ran up and said, "Come quick. The dragon is calling you."

Game to play: On Your Own

Ed and Mel are feeling a bit overwhelmed with everything that has happened. Try not to get overwhelmed in this word game.

Materials needed:
-   Game cards and tally recording sheet. See Game Appendix.

Rules:
1. Shuffle the cards and make a draw pile.
2. Player One will draw a card and read the word. Player One and Player Two need to remember the word. Put the card into a discard pile where it can't be seen.
3. Player Two will draw a card and read the word. Player Two needs to say the first word and the new word in order. Player One and Player Two need to remember both words. Players do **not** help each other remember the words. Put the card into a discard pile where it can't be seen.
4. Player One draws another card to read. They will need to say the first two words and the new word in order.
5. Player Two draws another card to read. They will need to say the first three words and the new word in order.
6. Play continues until someone can't remember the words in order. If the other player can remember all the words in order at that point, they win the game.
7. **IMPORTANT!** Mark down the number of words that each player can remember in order. This number will be referred to in the next game.

Chapter 15

Narrator (Parent or Tutor):

Ed and Mel picked themselves up and went to see the dragon. She seemed to be getting worse, but she was making noise and trying to move. She settled down a bit once Ed and Mel sat down with her. She began to grumble and huff.

Jax began to translate the dragon's labored speech. "She doesn't think she has much longer to live. She wants to share some important things with you first. Are you listening closely?"

Ed and Mel nodded their heads yes.

Jax continued to translate. "Thank you for saving my kin. We are thankful to not be fighting R. L. alone. Times are tough, but you must remember this, 'Seek wisdom.'

"Wisdom will help you understand your strengths and weaknesses. It will become a shield and watch over you through your successes . . . and your failures. Wisdom does not get its value through wins and losses. It has its value from truth, honesty, justice, and loyalty. Darkness, failure, and evil . . . these things can never steal its worth.

"Wisdom will shine light into the darkness so you can see the good. Evil shies away from Wisdom, as it shows evil for what it really is.

"Wisdom will learn from failure and grow. It can't be destroyed by failure. Wisdom will help you be refined through failure. It will help you ask questions, find new strategies, see the true goals, and not give up on them.

"Ed and Mel, the truth is you have given your whole selves with your strengths and weaknesses to get justice for Ebrin. You have loved us with what you have done. The value of that is not worthless. It is priceless. Nothing can destroy that. You and your family will always belong with us, even if we must leave Ebrin behind in ruins. We stand behind you and pray you continue to stand with us. Don't give up. Let Wisdom guide you."

Dad turned to Ed and Mel. He said, "That is how Mom and I feel too. No matter what happens, we are so proud of the people you two are becoming. Nothing can take away the love and courage you have shown. You have put others above yourselves and your difficulties. You haven't given up in fighting the spell. You learn a little more each day. The truth is nothing will change our love for you two. Nothing."

Ed took a deep breath, and Mel nodded. Jax could see their despair being chased away by acceptance and love.

The dragon continued with Jax's help. "Ebrin still needs you. Dragons can no longer live in your world, as a toxin there will eventually kill them. The babies need a medicine. You will have to search Ebrin for the ingredients to make the cure for the babies. The instructions must be followed exactly. Doc will give them to you. You will have to be careful, as this medicine will be toxic to you. Once you have it, go save the babies. Then, stop R. L. from coming back. And remember, whether you succeed or fail, we are with you."

Student text:

"We will!" Mel said. "We will keep in mind all you said and bring the two baby dragons back." She put her hand on the dragon's neck. "Please rest. Don't you quit. We do love Ebrin, its people, and the Felkin. That is why it is so difficult. That is also why we will not quit."

Ed did agree, "Thank you, my sweet dragon. I will listen to you. Thank you, Dad and Mom."

Ed did continue, "Wisdom will help me keep in mind that Mel and I have our family back, and the spell will not crush us."

Mel said, "We also met Jax, Ash, the Ebrin people, and the Felkin."

Ed did agree, "Yes, we have our family and friends. My family and friends love me even when I fail. I shouldn't think I am rubbish because of R. L. and this spell. I shouldn't think I'm rubbish because I didn't hit my goal yet. I haven't lost unless I quit.

"Rest now, dragon. We will find the baby dragons."

The dragon did moan as it began to relax again. It quickly fell asleep.

"Mom and Dad, do you still have that map of the rifts and the scroll?" Ed did ask. "I think I have a plan."

Epilogue

Narrator (Parent or Tutor):

Life can be full of irony. R. L.'s plan to avoid problems created his biggest problem. Ed, Mel, and Jax's plan to stop R. L. isn't going as they planned, either. There are bigger problems now as R. L. has the baby dragons, and Ebrin will eventually be turned into rubble. You could say they got out of the frying pan and into the fire. That is another way to say things went from bad to worse.

Ed, Mel, and Jax's grit, determination, and strengths are being tested by these unexpected and ironic twists. Fire has the ability to destroy and burn. But as the Felkin know, fire is what refines gold and strengthens iron. Again, it is ironic that what can burn and destroy can also refine and strengthen. The Felkin believe this challenge will refine and strengthen Ed and Mel.

Though they are beaten and bruised, Ed and Mel will take what they have learned and see this hunt, and now rescue, through to the end. If you can relate to their difficulties, take courage. The story is not over.

Game to play: Better Together

The dragon wants Ed and Mel to remember the bigger picture. It is wise to look at our strengths and weaknesses, struggles and triumphs in the context of our character and community. There was a certain amount of words you could remember in the game "On Your Own." These words were randomly drawn from a stack of cards. See how context and teamwork changes the number of words you can remember.

Materials needed:

- Game sentences and Sentence Frame. See Game Appendix.

Rules:

1. Select a passage to read.
2. Player One will read the first sentence using the page with a cutout (Sentence Frame) to cover all the sentences but the line that is being read. The sentence may be read multiple times.
3. Player One and Player Two need to remember the sentence.
4. Player Two will read the next sentence using the cutout.
5. Player Two needs to say sentence number one and sentence number two without looking at them. Player One and Player Two can help each other remember the correct wording.
6. Player One will read sentence number three and repeat the process.
7. When the sentences can't be remembered with help from either player, stop and count the number of words remembered. Each sentence has a number at the end to help you tally up the number of words. This number is a team number. Compare the number of words remembered to the words remembered in the game "On Your Own." How is the number different?

Resource Appendix:

Game Tokens:

Many different household items can be used for the various games such as dried beans, colored buttons, and more. The transparent counting chips that are mentioned also work well. Here is an example of the transparent counting chips. (I do not receive any commission from or have an association with this company.)

https://www.amazon.com/Learning-Resources-Transparent-Counting-Assorted/dp/B00004WKPM/ref=sr_1_7?keywords=colored+math+markers&qid=1572463721&sr=8-7

Syllable division rules:

The following information about syllable division is for readers who are NOT using the Barton Reading & Spelling System.

https://sarahsnippets.com/syllable-division-rules/ This link has a lot of information about syllable division. There is some information here that is addressed in later Barton Reading & Spelling System levels, such as suffixes and dividing between two vowels. This link will have the information you will need to play the syllable division games. I want to highlight one exception for dividing the VCCV pattern. The page at this link mentions an exception to the rule when "R" is the second consonant. The games in this book also use "L" as an exception to this division rule. Also, these exceptions do not work 100% of the time. R's and L's can be a bit bothersome in syllable division. Hmm, R and L, why does that sound familiar?

Schwa:

The Barton Reading & Spelling System has a good approach to teaching students about the schwa sound. As a parent of a Barton student and as a tutor, I appreciate the way it is addressed within the program.

The following information about schwa is for readers who are <u>NOT</u> using the Barton Reading & Spelling System.

Here are some websites and videos that discuss schwa:
- **https://blog.logicofenglish.com/what-is-a-schwa-helping-students-read-and-spell-the-schwa-sound**

- **https://blog.logicofenglish.com/the-clever-monks-why-o-sometimes-says-short-u**

- **https://blog.allaboutlearningpress.com/schwas/**

- "The Great Australian Schwa" - **https://youtu.be/e9YghG6klUk**

Accents and schwa:
- From Logic of English – **https://youtu.be/Cg3SwAo5iw8**

Game Appendix:

NOTE: A PDF of the Game Appendix can be found at DecodableAdventures.com under the "eBook Users" page.

Also, check the "eBook Users" page for links to alternate digital formats for some games.

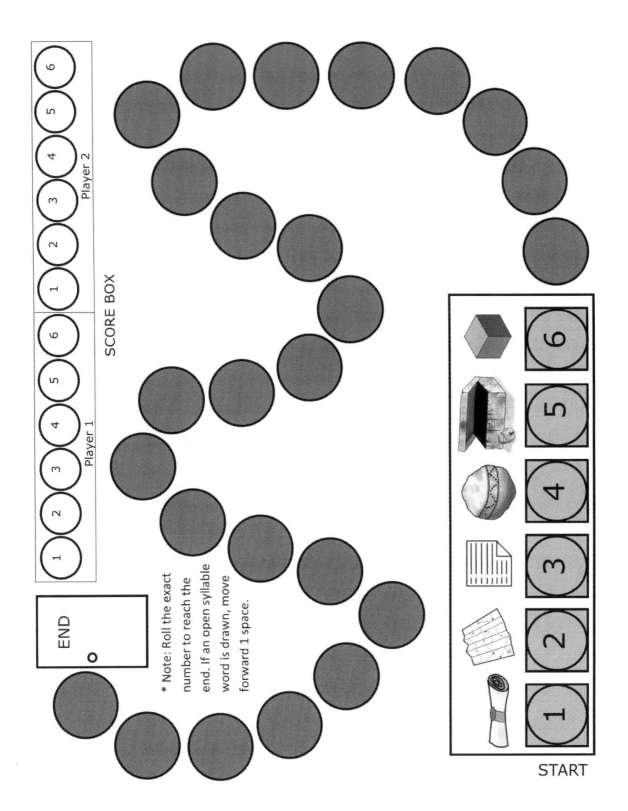

SCORE BOX

Player 2

| 1 | 2 | 3 | 4 | 5 | 6 |

Player 1

| 1 | 2 | 3 | 4 | 5 | 6 |

END
○

* Note: Roll the exact number to reach the end. If an open syllable word is drawn, move forward 1 space.

START

117

1 1 1 1 1 1 1 1 1 1 1 1 1 1 1 1 1 1 1 1 1 1 1 1 1 1 1 1 1 1 1 1 1 1 1 1 1 1 1 1
1 1 1 1 1 1 1 1 1 1 1 1 1 1 1 1 1 1 1 1 1 1 1 1 1 1 1 1 1 1 1 1 1 1 1 1 1 1 1 1
1 1 1 1 1 1 1 1 1 1 1 1 1 1 1 1 1 1 1 1 1 1 1 1 1 1 1 1 1 1 1 1 1 1 1 1 1 1 1 1
1 1 1 1 1 1 1 1 1 1 1 1 1 1 1 1 1 1 1 1 1 1 1 1 1 1 1 1 1 1 1 1 1 1 1 1 1 1 1 1
1 1 1 1 1 1 1 1 1 1 1 1 1 1 1 1 1 1 1 1 1 1 1 1 1 1 1 1 1 1 1 1 1 1 1 1 1 1 1 1
1 1 1 1 1 1 1 1 1 1 1 1 1 1 1 1 1 1 1 1 1 1 1 1 1 1 1 1 1 1 1 1 1 1 1 1 1 1 1 1
1 1 1 1 1 1 1 1 1 1 1 1 1 1 1 1 1 1 1 1 1 1 1 1 1 1 1 1 1 1 1 1 1 1 1 1 1 1 1 1
1 1 1 1 1 1 1 1 1 1 1 1 1 1 1 1 1 1 1 1 1 1 1 1 1 1 1 1 1 1 1 1 1 1 1 1 1 1 1 1
1 1 1 1 1 1 1 1 1 1 1 1 1 1 1 1 1 1 1 1 1 1 1 1 1 1 1 1 1 1 1 1 1 1 1 1 1 1 1 1
1 1 1 1 1 1 1 1 1 1 1 1 1 1 1 1 1 1 1 1 1 1 1 1 1 1 1 1 1 1 1 1 1 1 1 1 1 1 1 1
1 1 1 1 1 1 1 1 1 1 1 1 1 1 1 1 1 1 1 1 1 1 1 1 1 1 1 1 1 1 1 1 1 1 1 1 1 1 1 1
1 1 1 1 1 1 1 1 1 1 1 1 1 1 1 1 1 1 1 1 1 1 1 1 1 1 1 1 1 1 1 1 1 1 1 1 1 1 1 1
1 1 1 1 1 1 1 1 1 1 1 1 1 1 1 1 1 1 1 1 1 1 1 1 1 1 1 1 1 1 1 1 1 1 1 1 1 1 1 1
1 1 1 1 1 1 1 1 1 1 1 1 1 1 1 1 1 1 1 1 1 1 1 1 1 1 1 1 1 1 1 1 1 1 1 1 1 1 1 1
1 1 1 1 1 1 1 1 1 1 1 1 1 1 1 1 1 1 1 1 1 1 1 1 1 1 1 1 1 1 1 1 1 1 1 1 1 1 1 1
1 1 1 1 1 1 1 1 1 1 1 1 1 1 1 1 1 1 1 1 1 1 1 1 1 1 1 1 1 1 1 1 1 1 1 1 1 1 1 1
1 1 1 1 1 1 1 1 1 1 1 1 1 1 1 1 1 1 1 1 1 1 1 1 1 1 1 1 1 1 1 1 1 1 1 1 1 1 1 1
1 1 1 1 1 1 1 1 1 1 1 1 1 1 1 1 1 1 1 1 1 1 1 1 1 1 1 1 1 1 1 1 1 1 1 1 1 1 1 1
1 1 1 1 1 1 1 1 1 1 1 1 1 1 1 1 1 1 1 1 1 1 1 1 1 1 1 1 1 1 1 1 1 1 1 1 1 1 1 1
1 1 1 1 1 1 1 1 1 1 1 1 1 1 1 1 1 1 1 1 1 1 1 1 1 1 1 1 1 1 1 1 1 1 1 1 1 1 1 1
1 1 1 1 1 1 1 1 1 1 1 1 1 1 1 1 1 1 1 1 1 1 1 1 1 1 1 1 1 1 1 1 1 1 1 1 1 1 1 1
1 1 1 1 1 1 1 1 1 1 1 1 1 1 1 1 1 1 1 1 1 1 1 1 1 1 1 1 1 1 1 1 1 1 1 1 1 1 1 1
1 1 1 1 1 1 1 1 1 1 1 1 1 1 1 1 1 1 1 1 1 1 1 1 1 1 1 1 1 1 1 1 1 1 1 1 1 1 1 1
1 1 1 1 1 1 1 1 1 1 1 1 1 1 1 1 1 1 1 1 1 1 1 1 1 1 1 1 1 1 1 1 1 1 1 1 1 1 1 1
1 1 1 1 1 1 1 1 1 1 1 1 1 1 1 1 1 1 1 1 1 1 1 1 1 1 1 1 1 1 1 1 1 1 1 1 1 1 1 1
1 1 1 1 1 1 1 1 1 1 1 1 1 1 1 1 1 1 1 1 1 1 1 1 1 1 1 1 1 1 1 1 1 1 1 1 1 1 1 1
1 1 1 1 1 1 1 1 1 1 1 1 1 1 1 1 1 1 1 1 1 1 1 1 1 1 1 1 1 1 1 1 1 1 1 1 1 1 1 1
1 1 1 1 1 1 1 1 1 1 1 1 1 1 1 1 1 1 1 1 1 1 1 1 1 1 1 1 1 1 1 1 1 1 1 1 1 1 1 1
1 1 1 1 1 1 1 1 1 1 1 1 1 1 1 1 1 1 1 1 1 1 1 1 1 1 1 1 1 1 1 1 1 1 1 1 1 1 1 1
1 1 1 1 1 1 1 1 1 1 1 1 1 1 1 1 1 1 1 1 1 1 1 1 1 1 1 1 1 1 1 1 1 1 1 1 1 1 1 1

he	she	we	<u>so</u>
go	hi	<u>no</u>	my
why	try	fly	shy
sky	spy	fry	flu

1 1 1 1 1 1 1 1 1 1 1 1 1 1 1 1 1 1 1 1 1 1 1 1 1 1 1 1 1 1 1 1 1 1 1 1 1 1 1 1
1 1 1 1 1 1 1 1 1 1 1 1 1 1 1 1 1 1 1 1 1 1 1 1 1 1 1 1 1 1 1 1 1 1 1 1 1 1 1 1
1 1 1 1 1 1 1 1 1 1 1 1 1 1 1 1 1 1 1 1 1 1 1 1 1 1 1 1 1 1 1 1 1 1 1 1 1 1 1 1
1 1 1 1 1 1 1 1 1 1 1 1 1 1 1 1 1 1 1 1 1 1 1 1 1 1 1 1 1 1 1 1 1 1 1 1 1 1 1 1
1 1 1 1 1 1 1 1 1 1 1 1 1 1 1 1 1 1 1 1 1 1 1 1 1 1 1 1 1 1 1 1 1 1 1 1 1 1 1 1
1 1 1 1 1 1 1 1 1 1 1 1 1 1 1 1 1 1 1 1 1 1 1 1 1 1 1 1 1 1 1 1 1 1 1 1 1 1 1 1
1 1 1 1 1 1 1 1 1 1 1 1 1 1 1 1 1 1 1 1 1 1 1 1 1 1 1 1 1 1 1 1 1 1 1 1 1 1 1 1
1 1 1 1 1 1 1 1 1 1 1 1 1 1 1 1 1 1 1 1 1 1 1 1 1 1 1 1 1 1 1 1 1 1 1 1 1 1 1 1
1 1 1 1 1 1 1 1 1 1 1 1 1 1 1 1 1 1 1 1 1 1 1 1 1 1 1 1 1 1 1 1 1 1 1 1 1 1 1 1
1 1 1 1 1 1 1 1 1 1 1 1 1 1 1 1 1 1 1 1 1 1 1 1 1 1 1 1 1 1 1 1 1 1 1 1 1 1 1 1
1 1 1 1 1 1 1 1 1 1 1 1 1 1 1 1 1 1 1 1 1 1 1 1 1 1 1 1 1 1 1 1 1 1 1 1 1 1 1 1
1 1 1 1 1 1 1 1 1 1 1 1 1 1 1 1 1 1 1 1 1 1 1 1 1 1 1 1 1 1 1 1 1 1 1 1 1 1 1 1
1 1 1 1 1 1 1 1 1 1 1 1 1 1 1 1 1 1 1 1 1 1 1 1 1 1 1 1 1 1 1 1 1 1 1 1 1 1 1 1
1 1 1 1 1 1 1 1 1 1 1 1 1 1 1 1 1 1 1 1 1 1 1 1 1 1 1 1 1 1 1 1 1 1 1 1 1 1 1 1
1 1 1 1 1 1 1 1 1 1 1 1 1 1 1 1 1 1 1 1 1 1 1 1 1 1 1 1 1 1 1 1 1 1 1 1 1 1 1 1
1 1 1 1 1 1 1 1 1 1 1 1 1 1 1 1 1 1 1 1 1 1 1 1 1 1 1 1 1 1 1 1 1 1 1 1 1 1 1 1
1 1 1 1 1 1 1 1 1 1 1 1 1 1 1 1 1 1 1 1 1 1 1 1 1 1 1 1 1 1 1 1 1 1 1 1 1 1 1 1
1 1 1 1 1 1 1 1 1 1 1 1 1 1 1 1 1 1 1 1 1 1 1 1 1 1 1 1 1 1 1 1 1 1 1 1 1 1 1 1
1 1 1 1 1 1 1 1 1 1 1 1 1 1 1 1 1 1 1 1 1 1 1 1 1 1 1 1 1 1 1 1 1 1 1 1 1 1 1 1
1 1 1 1 1 1 1 1 1 1 1 1 1 1 1 1 1 1 1 1 1 1 1 1 1 1 1 1 1 1 1 1 1 1 1 1 1 1 1 1
1 1 1 1 1 1 1 1 1 1 1 1 1 1 1 1 1 1 1 1 1 1 1 1 1 1 1 1 1 1 1 1 1 1 1 1 1 1 1 1
1 1 1 1 1 1 1 1 1 1 1 1 1 1 1 1 1 1 1 1 1 1 1 1 1 1 1 1 1 1 1 1 1 1 1 1 1 1 1 1
1 1 1 1 1 1 1 1 1 1 1 1 1 1 1 1 1 1 1 1 1 1 1 1 1 1 1 1 1 1 1 1 1 1 1 1 1 1 1 1
1 1 1 1 1 1 1 1 1 1 1 1 1 1 1 1 1 1 1 1 1 1 1 1 1 1 1 1 1 1 1 1 1 1 1 1 1 1 1 1
1 1 1 1 1 1 1 1 1 1 1 1 1 1 1 1 1 1 1 1 1 1 1 1 1 1 1 1 1 1 1 1 1 1 1 1 1 1 1 1
1 1 1 1 1 1 1 1 1 1 1 1 1 1 1 1 1 1 1 1 1 1 1 1 1 1 1 1 1 1 1 1 1 1 1 1 1 1 1 1
1 1 1 1 1 1 1 1 1 1 1 1 1 1 1 1 1 1 1 1 1 1 1 1 1 1 1 1 1 1 1 1 1 1 1 1 1 1 1 1
1 1 1 1 1 1 1 1 1 1 1 1 1 1 1 1 1 1 1 1 1 1 1 1 1 1 1 1 1 1 1 1 1 1 1 1 1 1 1 1
1 1 1 1 1 1 1 1 1 1 1 1 1 1 1 1 1 1 1 1 1 1 1 1 1 1 1 1 1 1 1 1 1 1 1 1 1 1 1 1
1 1 1 1 1 1 1 1 1 1 1 1 1 1 1 1 1 1 1 1 1 1 1 1 1 1 1 1 1 1 1 1 1 1 1 1 1 1 1 1
1 1 1 1 1 1 1 1 1 1 1 1 1 1 1 1 1 1 1 1 1 1 1 1 1 1 1 1 1 1 1 1 1 1 1 1 1 1 1 1
1 1 1 1 1 1 1 1 1 1 1 1 1 1 1 1 1 1 1 1 1 1 1 1 1 1 1 1 1 1 1 1 1 1 1 1 1 1 1 1
1 1 1 1 1 1 1 1 1 1 1 1 1 1 1 1 1 1 1 1 1 1 1 1 1 1 1 1 1 1 1 1 1 1 1 1 1 1 1 1
1 1 1 1 1 1 1 1 1 1 1 1 1 1 1 1 1 1 1 1 1 1 1 1 1 1 1 1 1 1 1 1 1 1 1 1 1 1 1 1

bench	jump	fluff	went
hand	long	best	bet
squint	spot	think	match
pop	land	crack	tell

1 1 1 1 1 1 1 1 1 1 1 1 1 1 1 1 1 1 1 1 1 1 1 1 1 1 1 1 1 1 1 1 1 1 1
1 1 1 1 1 1 1 1 1 1 1 1 1 1 1 1 1 1 1 1 1 1 1 1 1 1 1 1 1 1 1 1 1 1 1
1 1 1 1 1 1 1 1 1 1 1 1 1 1 1 1 1 1 1 1 1 1 1 1 1 1 1 1 1 1 1 1 1 1 1
1 1 1 1 1 1 1 1 1 1 1 1 1 1 1 1 1 1 1 1 1 1 1 1 1 1 1 1 1 1 1 1 1 1 1
1 1 1 1 1 1 1 1 1 1 1 1 1 1 1 1 1 1 1 1 1 1 1 1 1 1 1 1 1 1 1 1 1 1 1
1 1 1 1 1 1 1 1 1 1 1 1 1 1 1 1 1 1 1 1 1 1 1 1 1 1 1 1 1 1 1 1 1 1 1
1 1 1 1 1 1 1 1 1 1 1 1 1 1 1 1 1 1 1 1 1 1 1 1 1 1 1 1 1 1 1 1 1 1 1
1 1 1 1 1 1 1 1 1 1 1 1 1 1 1 1 1 1 1 1 1 1 1 1 1 1 1 1 1 1 1 1 1 1 1
1 1 1 1 1 1 1 1 1 1 1 1 1 1 1 1 1 1 1 1 1 1 1 1 1 1 1 1 1 1 1 1 1 1 1
1 1 1 1 1 1 1 1 1 1 1 1 1 1 1 1 1 1 1 1 1 1 1 1 1 1 1 1 1 1 1 1 1 1 1
1 1 1 1 1 1 1 1 1 1 1 1 1 1 1 1 1 1 1 1 1 1 1 1 1 1 1 1 1 1 1 1 1 1 1
1 1 1 1 1 1 1 1 1 1 1 1 1 1 1 1 1 1 1 1 1 1 1 1 1 1 1 1 1 1 1 1 1 1 1
1 1 1 1 1 1 1 1 1 1 1 1 1 1 1 1 1 1 1 1 1 1 1 1 1 1 1 1 1 1 1 1 1 1 1
1 1 1 1 1 1 1 1 1 1 1 1 1 1 1 1 1 1 1 1 1 1 1 1 1 1 1 1 1 1 1 1 1 1 1
1 1 1 1 1 1 1 1 1 1 1 1 1 1 1 1 1 1 1 1 1 1 1 1 1 1 1 1 1 1 1 1 1 1 1
1 1 1 1 1 1 1 1 1 1 1 1 1 1 1 1 1 1 1 1 1 1 1 1 1 1 1 1 1 1 1 1 1 1 1
1 1 1 1 1 1 1 1 1 1 1 1 1 1 1 1 1 1 1 1 1 1 1 1 1 1 1 1 1 1 1 1 1 1 1
1 1 1 1 1 1 1 1 1 1 1 1 1 1 1 1 1 1 1 1 1 1 1 1 1 1 1 1 1 1 1 1 1 1 1
1 1 1 1 1 1 1 1 1 1 1 1 1 1 1 1 1 1 1 1 1 1 1 1 1 1 1 1 1 1 1 1 1 1 1
1 1 1 1 1 1 1 1 1 1 1 1 1 1 1 1 1 1 1 1 1 1 1 1 1 1 1 1 1 1 1 1 1 1 1
1 1 1 1 1 1 1 1 1 1 1 1 1 1 1 1 1 1 1 1 1 1 1 1 1 1 1 1 1 1 1 1 1 1 1
1 1 1 1 1 1 1 1 1 1 1 1 1 1 1 1 1 1 1 1 1 1 1 1 1 1 1 1 1 1 1 1 1 1 1
1 1 1 1 1 1 1 1 1 1 1 1 1 1 1 1 1 1 1 1 1 1 1 1 1 1 1 1 1 1 1 1 1 1 1
1 1 1 1 1 1 1 1 1 1 1 1 1 1 1 1 1 1 1 1 1 1 1 1 1 1 1 1 1 1 1 1 1 1 1
1 1 1 1 1 1 1 1 1 1 1 1 1 1 1 1 1 1 1 1 1 1 1 1 1 1 1 1 1 1 1 1 1 1 1
1 1 1 1 1 1 1 1 1 1 1 1 1 1 1 1 1 1 1 1 1 1 1 1 1 1 1 1 1 1 1 1 1 1 1
1 1 1 1 1 1 1 1 1 1 1 1 1 1 1 1 1 1 1 1 1 1 1 1 1 1 1 1 1 1 1 1 1 1 1
1 1 1 1 1 1 1 1 1 1 1 1 1 1 1 1 1 1 1 1 1 1 1 1 1 1 1 1 1 1 1 1 1 1 1
1 1 1 1 1 1 1 1 1 1 1 1 1 1 1 1 1 1 1 1 1 1 1 1 1 1 1 1 1 1 1 1 1 1 1
1 1 1 1 1 1 1 1 1 1 1 1 1 1 1 1 1 1 1 1 1 1 1 1 1 1 1 1 1 1 1 1 1 1 1

scroll	map	list	gold
box	block	roll	cast
<u>us</u>	rift	six	off
shell	hold	quick	must

1 1 1 1 1 1 1 1 1 1 1 1 1 1 1 1 1 1 1 1 1 1 1 1 1 1 1 1 1 1 1 1 1 1 1 1 1 1 1 1 1 1
1 1 1 1 1 1 1 1 1 1 1 1 1 1 1 1 1 1 1 1 1 1 1 1 1 1 1 1 1 1 1 1 1 1 1 1 1 1 1 1 1 1
1 1 1 1 1 1 1 1 1 1 1 1 1 1 1 1 1 1 1 1 1 1 1 1 1 1 1 1 1 1 1 1 1 1 1 1 1 1 1 1 1 1
1 1 1 1 1 1 1 1 1 1 1 1 1 1 1 1 1 1 1 1 1 1 1 1 1 1 1 1 1 1 1 1 1 1 1 1 1 1 1 1 1 1
1 1 1 1 1 1 1 1 1 1 1 1 1 1 1 1 1 1 1 1 1 1 1 1 1 1 1 1 1 1 1 1 1 1 1 1 1 1 1 1 1 1
1 1 1 1 1 1 1 1 1 1 1 1 1 1 1 1 1 1 1 1 1 1 1 1 1 1 1 1 1 1 1 1 1 1 1 1 1 1 1 1 1 1
1 1 1 1 1 1 1 1 1 1 1 1 1 1 1 1 1 1 1 1 1 1 1 1 1 1 1 1 1 1 1 1 1 1 1 1 1 1 1 1 1 1
1 1 1 1 1 1 1 1 1 1 1 1 1 1 1 1 1 1 1 1 1 1 1 1 1 1 1 1 1 1 1 1 1 1 1 1 1 1 1 1 1 1
1 1 1 1 1 1 1 1 1 1 1 1 1 1 1 1 1 1 1 1 1 1 1 1 1 1 1 1 1 1 1 1 1 1 1 1 1 1 1 1 1 1
1 1 1 1 1 1 1 1 1 1 1 1 1 1 1 1 1 1 1 1 1 1 1 1 1 1 1 1 1 1 1 1 1 1 1 1 1 1 1 1 1 1
1 1 1 1 1 1 1 1 1 1 1 1 1 1 1 1 1 1 1 1 1 1 1 1 1 1 1 1 1 1 1 1 1 1 1 1 1 1 1 1 1 1
1 1 1 1 1 1 1 1 1 1 1 1 1 1 1 1 1 1 1 1 1 1 1 1 1 1 1 1 1 1 1 1 1 1 1 1 1 1 1 1 1 1
1 1 1 1 1 1 1 1 1 1 1 1 1 1 1 1 1 1 1 1 1 1 1 1 1 1 1 1 1 1 1 1 1 1 1 1 1 1 1 1 1 1
1 1 1 1 1 1 1 1 1 1 1 1 1 1 1 1 1 1 1 1 1 1 1 1 1 1 1 1 1 1 1 1 1 1 1 1 1 1 1 1 1 1
1 1 1 1 1 1 1 1 1 1 1 1 1 1 1 1 1 1 1 1 1 1 1 1 1 1 1 1 1 1 1 1 1 1 1 1 1 1 1 1 1 1
1 1 1 1 1 1 1 1 1 1 1 1 1 1 1 1 1 1 1 1 1 1 1 1 1 1 1 1 1 1 1 1 1 1 1 1 1 1 1 1 1 1
1 1 1 1 1 1 1 1 1 1 1 1 1 1 1 1 1 1 1 1 1 1 1 1 1 1 1 1 1 1 1 1 1 1 1 1 1 1 1 1 1 1
1 1 1 1 1 1 1 1 1 1 1 1 1 1 1 1 1 1 1 1 1 1 1 1 1 1 1 1 1 1 1 1 1 1 1 1 1 1 1 1 1 1
1 1 1 1 1 1 1 1 1 1 1 1 1 1 1 1 1 1 1 1 1 1 1 1 1 1 1 1 1 1 1 1 1 1 1 1 1 1 1 1 1 1
1 1 1 1 1 1 1 1 1 1 1 1 1 1 1 1 1 1 1 1 1 1 1 1 1 1 1 1 1 1 1 1 1 1 1 1 1 1 1 1 1 1
1 1 1 1 1 1 1 1 1 1 1 1 1 1 1 1 1 1 1 1 1 1 1 1 1 1 1 1 1 1 1 1 1 1 1 1 1 1 1 1 1 1
1 1 1 1 1 1 1 1 1 1 1 1 1 1 1 1 1 1 1 1 1 1 1 1 1 1 1 1 1 1 1 1 1 1 1 1 1 1 1 1 1 1
1 1 1 1 1 1 1 1 1 1 1 1 1 1 1 1 1 1 1 1 1 1 1 1 1 1 1 1 1 1 1 1 1 1 1 1 1 1 1 1 1 1
1 1 1 1 1 1 1 1 1 1 1 1 1 1 1 1 1 1 1 1 1 1 1 1 1 1 1 1 1 1 1 1 1 1 1 1 1 1 1 1 1 1
1 1 1 1 1 1 1 1 1 1 1 1 1 1 1 1 1 1 1 1 1 1 1 1 1 1 1 1 1 1 1 1 1 1 1 1 1 1 1 1 1 1
1 1 1 1 1 1 1 1 1 1 1 1 1 1 1 1 1 1 1 1 1 1 1 1 1 1 1 1 1 1 1 1 1 1 1 1 1 1 1 1 1 1
1 1 1 1 1 1 1 1 1 1 1 1 1 1 1 1 1 1 1 1 1 1 1 1 1 1 1 1 1 1 1 1 1 1 1 1 1 1 1 1 1 1
1 1 1 1 1 1 1 1 1 1 1 1 1 1 1 1 1 1 1 1 1 1 1 1 1 1 1 1 1 1 1 1 1 1 1 1 1 1 1 1 1 1
1 1 1 1 1 1 1 1 1 1 1 1 1 1 1 1 1 1 1 1 1 1 1 1 1 1 1 1 1 1 1 1 1 1 1 1 1 1 1 1 1 1
1 1 1 1 1 1 1 1 1 1 1 1 1 1 1 1 1 1 1 1 1 1 1 1 1 1 1 1 1 1 1 1 1 1 1 1 1 1 1 1 1 1
1 1 1 1 1 1 1 1 1 1 1 1 1 1 1 1 1 1 1 1 1 1 1 1 1 1 1 1 1 1 1 1 1 1 1 1 1 1 1 1 1 1
1 1 1 1 1 1 1 1 1 1 1 1 1 1 1 1 1 1 1 1 1 1 1 1 1 1 1 1 1 1 1 1 1 1 1 1 1 1 1 1 1 1
1 1 1 1 1 1 1 1 1 1 1 1 1 1 1 1 1 1 1 1 1 1 1 1 1 1 1 1 1 1 1 1 1 1 1 1 1 1 1 1 1 1

If the consonant in the middle is in the end syllable in the real word

Add another point (+1).

Read the word with the syllable division that makes a real word.

Draw Pile

Read the word with the middle consonant to the end FIRST.

Earn a point (+1)

Player 2 points

Player 1 points

125

2 2 2 2 2 2 2 2 2 2 2 2 2 2 2 2 2 2 2 2 2 2 2 2 2 2 2 2 2 2 2 2 2
2 2 2 2 2 2 2 2 2 2 2 2 2 2 2 2 2 2 2 2 2 2 2 2 2 2 2 2 2 2 2 2 2
2 2 2 2 2 2 2 2 2 2 2 2 2 2 2 2 2 2 2 2 2 2 2 2 2 2 2 2 2 2 2 2 2
2 2 2 2 2 2 2 2 2 2 2 2 2 2 2 2 2 2 2 2 2 2 2 2 2 2 2 2 2 2 2 2 2
2 2 2 2 2 2 2 2 2 2 2 2 2 2 2 2 2 2 2 2 2 2 2 2 2 2 2 2 2 2 2 2 2
2 2 2 2 2 2 2 2 2 2 2 2 2 2 2 2 2 2 2 2 2 2 2 2 2 2 2 2 2 2 2 2 2
2 2 2 2 2 2 2 2 2 2 2 2 2 2 2 2 2 2 2 2 2 2 2 2 2 2 2 2 2 2 2 2 2
2 2 2 2 2 2 2 2 2 2 2 2 2 2 2 2 2 2 2 2 2 2 2 2 2 2 2 2 2 2 2 2 2
2 2 2 2 2 2 2 2 2 2 2 2 2 2 2 2 2 2 2 2 2 2 2 2 2 2 2 2 2 2 2 2 2
2 2 2 2 2 2 2 2 2 2 2 2 2 2 2 2 2 2 2 2 2 2 2 2 2 2 2 2 2 2 2 2 2
2 2 2 2 2 2 2 2 2 2 2 2 2 2 2 2 2 2 2 2 2 2 2 2 2 2 2 2 2 2 2 2 2
2 2 2 2 2 2 2 2 2 2 2 2 2 2 2 2 2 2 2 2 2 2 2 2 2 2 2 2 2 2 2 2 2
2 2 2 2 2 2 2 2 2 2 2 2 2 2 2 2 2 2 2 2 2 2 2 2 2 2 2 2 2 2 2 2 2
2 2 2 2 2 2 2 2 2 2 2 2 2 2 2 2 2 2 2 2 2 2 2 2 2 2 2 2 2 2 2 2 2
2 2 2 2 2 2 2 2 2 2 2 2 2 2 2 2 2 2 2 2 2 2 2 2 2 2 2 2 2 2 2 2 2
2 2 2 2 2 2 2 2 2 2 2 2 2 2 2 2 2 2 2 2 2 2 2 2 2 2 2 2 2 2 2 2 2
2 2 2 2 2 2 2 2 2 2 2 2 2 2 2 2 2 2 2 2 2 2 2 2 2 2 2 2 2 2 2 2 2
2 2 2 2 2 2 2 2 2 2 2 2 2 2 2 2 2 2 2 2 2 2 2 2 2 2 2 2 2 2 2 2 2
2 2 2 2 2 2 2 2 2 2 2 2 2 2 2 2 2 2 2 2 2 2 2 2 2 2 2 2 2 2 2 2 2
2 2 2 2 2 2 2 2 2 2 2 2 2 2 2 2 2 2 2 2 2 2 2 2 2 2 2 2 2 2 2 2 2
2 2 2 2 2 2 2 2 2 2 2 2 2 2 2 2 2 2 2 2 2 2 2 2 2 2 2 2 2 2 2 2 2
2 2 2 2 2 2 2 2 2 2 2 2 2 2 2 2 2 2 2 2 2 2 2 2 2 2 2 2 2 2 2 2 2
2 2 2 2 2 2 2 2 2 2 2 2 2 2 2 2 2 2 2 2 2 2 2 2 2 2 2 2 2 2 2 2 2
2 2 2 2 2 2 2 2 2 2 2 2 2 2 2 2 2 2 2 2 2 2 2 2 2 2 2 2 2 2 2 2 2
2 2 2 2 2 2 2 2 2 2 2 2 2 2 2 2 2 2 2 2 2 2 2 2 2 2 2 2 2 2 2 2 2
2 2 2 2 2 2 2 2 2 2 2 2 2 2 2 2 2 2 2 2 2 2 2 2 2 2 2 2 2 2 2 2 2
2 2 2 2 2 2 2 2 2 2 2 2 2 2 2 2 2 2 2 2 2 2 2 2 2 2 2 2 2 2 2 2 2
2 2 2 2 2 2 2 2 2 2 2 2 2 2 2 2 2 2 2 2 2 2 2 2 2 2 2 2 2 2 2 2 2
2 2 2 2 2 2 2 2 2 2 2 2 2 2 2 2 2 2 2 2 2 2 2 2 2 2 2 2 2 2 2 2 2
2 2 2 2 2 2 2 2 2 2 2 2 2 2 2 2 2 2 2 2 2 2 2 2 2 2 2 2 2 2 2 2 2
2 2 2 2 2 2 2 2 2 2 2 2 2 2 2 2 2 2 2 2 2 2 2 2 2 2 2 2 2 2 2 2 2
2 2 2 2 2 2 2 2 2 2 2 2 2 2 2 2 2 2 2 2 2 2 2 2 2 2 2 2 2 2 2 2 2

truly	hotel	behind	silent
focus	motel	predict	pretend
totem	decent	recess	bonus
pony	student	chosen	cupid

2 2 2 2 2 2 2 2 2 2 2 2 2 2 2 2 2 2 2 2 2 2 2 2 2 2 2 2 2 2
2 2 2 2 2 2 2 2 2 2 2 2 2 2 2 2 2 2 2 2 2 2 2 2 2 2 2 2 2 2
2 2 2 2 2 2 2 2 2 2 2 2 2 2 2 2 2 2 2 2 2 2 2 2 2 2 2 2 2 2
2 2 2 2 2 2 2 2 2 2 2 2 2 2 2 2 2 2 2 2 2 2 2 2 2 2 2 2 2 2
2 2 2 2 2 2 2 2 2 2 2 2 2 2 2 2 2 2 2 2 2 2 2 2 2 2 2 2 2 2
2 2 2 2 2 2 2 2 2 2 2 2 2 2 2 2 2 2 2 2 2 2 2 2 2 2 2 2 2 2
2 2 2 2 2 2 2 2 2 2 2 2 2 2 2 2 2 2 2 2 2 2 2 2 2 2 2 2 2 2
2 2 2 2 2 2 2 2 2 2 2 2 2 2 2 2 2 2 2 2 2 2 2 2 2 2 2 2 2 2
2 2 2 2 2 2 2 2 2 2 2 2 2 2 2 2 2 2 2 2 2 2 2 2 2 2 2 2 2 2
2 2 2 2 2 2 2 2 2 2 2 2 2 2 2 2 2 2 2 2 2 2 2 2 2 2 2 2 2 2
2 2 2 2 2 2 2 2 2 2 2 2 2 2 2 2 2 2 2 2 2 2 2 2 2 2 2 2 2 2
2 2 2 2 2 2 2 2 2 2 2 2 2 2 2 2 2 2 2 2 2 2 2 2 2 2 2 2 2 2
2 2 2 2 2 2 2 2 2 2 2 2 2 2 2 2 2 2 2 2 2 2 2 2 2 2 2 2 2 2
2 2 2 2 2 2 2 2 2 2 2 2 2 2 2 2 2 2 2 2 2 2 2 2 2 2 2 2 2 2
2 2 2 2 2 2 2 2 2 2 2 2 2 2 2 2 2 2 2 2 2 2 2 2 2 2 2 2 2 2
2 2 2 2 2 2 2 2 2 2 2 2 2 2 2 2 2 2 2 2 2 2 2 2 2 2 2 2 2 2
2 2 2 2 2 2 2 2 2 2 2 2 2 2 2 2 2 2 2 2 2 2 2 2 2 2 2 2 2 2
2 2 2 2 2 2 2 2 2 2 2 2 2 2 2 2 2 2 2 2 2 2 2 2 2 2 2 2 2 2
2 2 2 2 2 2 2 2 2 2 2 2 2 2 2 2 2 2 2 2 2 2 2 2 2 2 2 2 2 2
2 2 2 2 2 2 2 2 2 2 2 2 2 2 2 2 2 2 2 2 2 2 2 2 2 2 2 2 2 2
2 2 2 2 2 2 2 2 2 2 2 2 2 2 2 2 2 2 2 2 2 2 2 2 2 2 2 2 2 2
2 2 2 2 2 2 2 2 2 2 2 2 2 2 2 2 2 2 2 2 2 2 2 2 2 2 2 2 2 2
2 2 2 2 2 2 2 2 2 2 2 2 2 2 2 2 2 2 2 2 2 2 2 2 2 2 2 2 2 2
2 2 2 2 2 2 2 2 2 2 2 2 2 2 2 2 2 2 2 2 2 2 2 2 2 2 2 2 2 2
2 2 2 2 2 2 2 2 2 2 2 2 2 2 2 2 2 2 2 2 2 2 2 2 2 2 2 2 2 2
2 2 2 2 2 2 2 2 2 2 2 2 2 2 2 2 2 2 2 2 2 2 2 2 2 2 2 2 2 2
2 2 2 2 2 2 2 2 2 2 2 2 2 2 2 2 2 2 2 2 2 2 2 2 2 2 2 2 2 2
2 2 2 2 2 2 2 2 2 2 2 2 2 2 2 2 2 2 2 2 2 2 2 2 2 2 2 2 2 2
2 2 2 2 2 2 2 2 2 2 2 2 2 2 2 2 2 2 2 2 2 2 2 2 2 2 2 2 2 2
2 2 2 2 2 2 2 2 2 2 2 2 2 2 2 2 2 2 2 2 2 2 2 2 2 2 2 2 2 2
2 2 2 2 2 2 2 2 2 2 2 2 2 2 2 2 2 2 2 2 2 2 2 2 2 2 2 2 2 2
2 2 2 2 2 2 2 2 2 2 2 2 2 2 2 2 2 2 2 2 2 2 2 2 2 2 2 2 2 2

began	open	even	robot
spoken	bacon	icy	ivy
vanish	lily	tulip	moment
study	copy	tiny	event

profit	robin	spiky	frozen
city	denim	virus	minus
planet	seven	request	basic
finish	radish	relax	taken

2 2 2 2 2 2 2 2 2 2 2 2 2 2 2 2 2 2 2 2 2 2 2 2 2 2 2 2 2 2 2 2 2 2 2
2 2 2 2 2 2 2 2 2 2 2 2 2 2 2 2 2 2 2 2 2 2 2 2 2 2 2 2 2 2 2 2 2 2 2
2 2 2 2 2 2 2 2 2 2 2 2 2 2 2 2 2 2 2 2 2 2 2 2 2 2 2 2 2 2 2 2 2 2 2
2 2 2 2 2 2 2 2 2 2 2 2 2 2 2 2 2 2 2 2 2 2 2 2 2 2 2 2 2 2 2 2 2 2 2
2 2 2 2 2 2 2 2 2 2 2 2 2 2 2 2 2 2 2 2 2 2 2 2 2 2 2 2 2 2 2 2 2 2 2
2 2 2 2 2 2 2 2 2 2 2 2 2 2 2 2 2 2 2 2 2 2 2 2 2 2 2 2 2 2 2 2 2 2 2
2 2 2 2 2 2 2 2 2 2 2 2 2 2 2 2 2 2 2 2 2 2 2 2 2 2 2 2 2 2 2 2 2 2 2
2 2 2 2 2 2 2 2 2 2 2 2 2 2 2 2 2 2 2 2 2 2 2 2 2 2 2 2 2 2 2 2 2 2 2
2 2 2 2 2 2 2 2 2 2 2 2 2 2 2 2 2 2 2 2 2 2 2 2 2 2 2 2 2 2 2 2 2 2 2
2 2 2 2 2 2 2 2 2 2 2 2 2 2 2 2 2 2 2 2 2 2 2 2 2 2 2 2 2 2 2 2 2 2 2
2 2 2 2 2 2 2 2 2 2 2 2 2 2 2 2 2 2 2 2 2 2 2 2 2 2 2 2 2 2 2 2 2 2 2
2 2 2 2 2 2 2 2 2 2 2 2 2 2 2 2 2 2 2 2 2 2 2 2 2 2 2 2 2 2 2 2 2 2 2
2 2 2 2 2 2 2 2 2 2 2 2 2 2 2 2 2 2 2 2 2 2 2 2 2 2 2 2 2 2 2 2 2 2 2
2 2 2 2 2 2 2 2 2 2 2 2 2 2 2 2 2 2 2 2 2 2 2 2 2 2 2 2 2 2 2 2 2 2 2
2 2 2 2 2 2 2 2 2 2 2 2 2 2 2 2 2 2 2 2 2 2 2 2 2 2 2 2 2 2 2 2 2 2 2
2 2 2 2 2 2 2 2 2 2 2 2 2 2 2 2 2 2 2 2 2 2 2 2 2 2 2 2 2 2 2 2 2 2 2
2 2 2 2 2 2 2 2 2 2 2 2 2 2 2 2 2 2 2 2 2 2 2 2 2 2 2 2 2 2 2 2 2 2 2
2 2 2 2 2 2 2 2 2 2 2 2 2 2 2 2 2 2 2 2 2 2 2 2 2 2 2 2 2 2 2 2 2 2 2
2 2 2 2 2 2 2 2 2 2 2 2 2 2 2 2 2 2 2 2 2 2 2 2 2 2 2 2 2 2 2 2 2 2 2
2 2 2 2 2 2 2 2 2 2 2 2 2 2 2 2 2 2 2 2 2 2 2 2 2 2 2 2 2 2 2 2 2 2 2
2 2 2 2 2 2 2 2 2 2 2 2 2 2 2 2 2 2 2 2 2 2 2 2 2 2 2 2 2 2 2 2 2 2 2
2 2 2 2 2 2 2 2 2 2 2 2 2 2 2 2 2 2 2 2 2 2 2 2 2 2 2 2 2 2 2 2 2 2 2
2 2 2 2 2 2 2 2 2 2 2 2 2 2 2 2 2 2 2 2 2 2 2 2 2 2 2 2 2 2 2 2 2 2 2
2 2 2 2 2 2 2 2 2 2 2 2 2 2 2 2 2 2 2 2 2 2 2 2 2 2 2 2 2 2 2 2 2 2 2
2 2 2 2 2 2 2 2 2 2 2 2 2 2 2 2 2 2 2 2 2 2 2 2 2 2 2 2 2 2 2 2 2 2 2
2 2 2 2 2 2 2 2 2 2 2 2 2 2 2 2 2 2 2 2 2 2 2 2 2 2 2 2 2 2 2 2 2 2 2
2 2 2 2 2 2 2 2 2 2 2 2 2 2 2 2 2 2 2 2 2 2 2 2 2 2 2 2 2 2 2 2 2 2 2
2 2 2 2 2 2 2 2 2 2 2 2 2 2 2 2 2 2 2 2 2 2 2 2 2 2 2 2 2 2 2 2 2 2 2
2 2 2 2 2 2 2 2 2 2 2 2 2 2 2 2 2 2 2 2 2 2 2 2 2 2 2 2 2 2 2 2 2 2 2
2 2 2 2 2 2 2 2 2 2 2 2 2 2 2 2 2 2 2 2 2 2 2 2 2 2 2 2 2 2 2 2 2 2 2
2 2 2 2 2 2 2 2 2 2 2 2 2 2 2 2 2 2 2 2 2 2 2 2 2 2 2 2 2 2 2 2 2 2 2

	pos					den
blink	net		sect		y	ty
nut	hot	sum	pen	den	meg	tab
sent	du	ket	et		con	net
up	ing	in	dog		kin	hap
	set	nas	pet	crick	ject	
ad	ab	plex	fin	let	bon	
	spunk	tist	mit	bas	sud	test
	mag	nap	muf	ob		trum

trumpet	basket	duplex	nutmeg
nasty	bonnet	napkin	cricket
admit	object	dentist	blinking
absent	muffin	magnet	happen
insect	tablet	sudden	contest
upset	hotdog	possum	spunky

3 3 3 3 3 3 3 3 3 3 3 3 3 3 3 3 3 3 3 3 3 3 3 3 3 3 3 3 3 3 3 3
3 3 3 3 3 3 3 3 3 3 3 3 3 3 3 3 3 3 3 3 3 3 3 3 3 3 3 3 3 3 3 3
3 3 3 3 3 3 3 3 3 3 3 3 3 3 3 3 3 3 3 3 3 3 3 3 3 3 3 3 3 3 3 3
3 3 3 3 3 3 3 3 3 3 3 3 3 3 3 3 3 3 3 3 3 3 3 3 3 3 3 3 3 3 3 3
3 3 3 3 3 3 3 3 3 3 3 3 3 3 3 3 3 3 3 3 3 3 3 3 3 3 3 3 3 3 3 3
3 3 3 3 3 3 3 3 3 3 3 3 3 3 3 3 3 3 3 3 3 3 3 3 3 3 3 3 3 3 3 3
3 3 3 3 3 3 3 3 3 3 3 3 3 3 3 3 3 3 3 3 3 3 3 3 3 3 3 3 3 3 3 3
3 3 3 3 3 3 3 3 3 3 3 3 3 3 3 3 3 3 3 3 3 3 3 3 3 3 3 3 3 3 3 3
3 3 3 3 3 3 3 3 3 3 3 3 3 3 3 3 3 3 3 3 3 3 3 3 3 3 3 3 3 3 3 3
3 3 3 3 3 3 3 3 3 3 3 3 3 3 3 3 3 3 3 3 3 3 3 3 3 3 3 3 3 3 3 3
3 3 3 3 3 3 3 3 3 3 3 3 3 3 3 3 3 3 3 3 3 3 3 3 3 3 3 3 3 3 3 3
3 3 3 3 3 3 3 3 3 3 3 3 3 3 3 3 3 3 3 3 3 3 3 3 3 3 3 3 3 3 3 3
3 3 3 3 3 3 3 3 3 3 3 3 3 3 3 3 3 3 3 3 3 3 3 3 3 3 3 3 3 3 3 3
3 3 3 3 3 3 3 3 3 3 3 3 3 3 3 3 3 3 3 3 3 3 3 3 3 3 3 3 3 3 3 3
3 3 3 3 3 3 3 3 3 3 3 3 3 3 3 3 3 3 3 3 3 3 3 3 3 3 3 3 3 3 3 3
3 3 3 3 3 3 3 3 3 3 3 3 3 3 3 3 3 3 3 3 3 3 3 3 3 3 3 3 3 3 3 3
3 3 3 3 3 3 3 3 3 3 3 3 3 3 3 3 3 3 3 3 3 3 3 3 3 3 3 3 3 3 3 3
3 3 3 3 3 3 3 3 3 3 3 3 3 3 3 3 3 3 3 3 3 3 3 3 3 3 3 3 3 3 3 3
3 3 3 3 3 3 3 3 3 3 3 3 3 3 3 3 3 3 3 3 3 3 3 3 3 3 3 3 3 3 3 3
3 3 3 3 3 3 3 3 3 3 3 3 3 3 3 3 3 3 3 3 3 3 3 3 3 3 3 3 3 3 3 3
3 3 3 3 3 3 3 3 3 3 3 3 3 3 3 3 3 3 3 3 3 3 3 3 3 3 3 3 3 3 3 3
3 3 3 3 3 3 3 3 3 3 3 3 3 3 3 3 3 3 3 3 3 3 3 3 3 3 3 3 3 3 3 3
3 3 3 3 3 3 3 3 3 3 3 3 3 3 3 3 3 3 3 3 3 3 3 3 3 3 3 3 3 3 3 3
3 3 3 3 3 3 3 3 3 3 3 3 3 3 3 3 3 3 3 3 3 3 3 3 3 3 3 3 3 3 3 3
3 3 3 3 3 3 3 3 3 3 3 3 3 3 3 3 3 3 3 3 3 3 3 3 3 3 3 3 3 3 3 3
3 3 3 3 3 3 3 3 3 3 3 3 3 3 3 3 3 3 3 3 3 3 3 3 3 3 3 3 3 3 3 3
3 3 3 3 3 3 3 3 3 3 3 3 3 3 3 3 3 3 3 3 3 3 3 3 3 3 3 3 3 3 3 3
3 3 3 3 3 3 3 3 3 3 3 3 3 3 3 3 3 3 3 3 3 3 3 3 3 3 3 3 3 3 3 3
3 3 3 3 3 3 3 3 3 3 3 3 3 3 3 3 3 3 3 3 3 3 3 3 3 3 3 3 3 3 3 3
3 3 3 3 3 3 3 3 3 3 3 3 3 3 3 3 3 3 3 3 3 3 3 3 3 3 3 3 3 3 3 3

open	open	closed	closed	open
open	open	closed	closed	closed
open	open	closed	closed	open

open	open	closed	closed	open
open	open	closed	closed	closed
open	open	closed	closed	open

locket	basket	he	we
nasty	bonnet	go	no
admit	object	why	fly
absent	muffin	sky	fry
insect	stricken	scruff	help
hectic	hotdog	lunch	tent

4 4 4 4 4 4 4 4 4 4 4 4 4 4 4 4 4 4 4 4 4 4 4 4 4 4 4 4 4 4 4 4
4 4 4 4 4 4 4 4 4 4 4 4 4 4 4 4 4 4 4 4 4 4 4 4 4 4 4 4 4 4 4 4
4 4 4 4 4 4 4 4 4 4 4 4 4 4 4 4 4 4 4 4 4 4 4 4 4 4 4 4 4 4 4 4
4 4 4 4 4 4 4 4 4 4 4 4 4 4 4 4 4 4 4 4 4 4 4 4 4 4 4 4 4 4 4 4
4 4 4 4 4 4 4 4 4 4 4 4 4 4 4 4 4 4 4 4 4 4 4 4 4 4 4 4 4 4 4 4
4 4 4 4 4 4 4 4 4 4 4 4 4 4 4 4 4 4 4 4 4 4 4 4 4 4 4 4 4 4 4 4
4 4 4 4 4 4 4 4 4 4 4 4 4 4 4 4 4 4 4 4 4 4 4 4 4 4 4 4 4 4 4 4
4 4 4 4 4 4 4 4 4 4 4 4 4 4 4 4 4 4 4 4 4 4 4 4 4 4 4 4 4 4 4 4
4 4 4 4 4 4 4 4 4 4 4 4 4 4 4 4 4 4 4 4 4 4 4 4 4 4 4 4 4 4 4 4
4 4 4 4 4 4 4 4 4 4 4 4 4 4 4 4 4 4 4 4 4 4 4 4 4 4 4 4 4 4 4 4
4 4 4 4 4 4 4 4 4 4 4 4 4 4 4 4 4 4 4 4 4 4 4 4 4 4 4 4 4 4 4 4
4 4 4 4 4 4 4 4 4 4 4 4 4 4 4 4 4 4 4 4 4 4 4 4 4 4 4 4 4 4 4 4
4 4 4 4 4 4 4 4 4 4 4 4 4 4 4 4 4 4 4 4 4 4 4 4 4 4 4 4 4 4 4 4
4 4 4 4 4 4 4 4 4 4 4 4 4 4 4 4 4 4 4 4 4 4 4 4 4 4 4 4 4 4 4 4
4 4 4 4 4 4 4 4 4 4 4 4 4 4 4 4 4 4 4 4 4 4 4 4 4 4 4 4 4 4 4 4
4 4 4 4 4 4 4 4 4 4 4 4 4 4 4 4 4 4 4 4 4 4 4 4 4 4 4 4 4 4 4 4
4 4 4 4 4 4 4 4 4 4 4 4 4 4 4 4 4 4 4 4 4 4 4 4 4 4 4 4 4 4 4 4
4 4 4 4 4 4 4 4 4 4 4 4 4 4 4 4 4 4 4 4 4 4 4 4 4 4 4 4 4 4 4 4
4 4 4 4 4 4 4 4 4 4 4 4 4 4 4 4 4 4 4 4 4 4 4 4 4 4 4 4 4 4 4 4
4 4 4 4 4 4 4 4 4 4 4 4 4 4 4 4 4 4 4 4 4 4 4 4 4 4 4 4 4 4 4 4
4 4 4 4 4 4 4 4 4 4 4 4 4 4 4 4 4 4 4 4 4 4 4 4 4 4 4 4 4 4 4 4
4 4 4 4 4 4 4 4 4 4 4 4 4 4 4 4 4 4 4 4 4 4 4 4 4 4 4 4 4 4 4 4
4 4 4 4 4 4 4 4 4 4 4 4 4 4 4 4 4 4 4 4 4 4 4 4 4 4 4 4 4 4 4 4
4 4 4 4 4 4 4 4 4 4 4 4 4 4 4 4 4 4 4 4 4 4 4 4 4 4 4 4 4 4 4 4
4 4 4 4 4 4 4 4 4 4 4 4 4 4 4 4 4 4 4 4 4 4 4 4 4 4 4 4 4 4 4 4
4 4 4 4 4 4 4 4 4 4 4 4 4 4 4 4 4 4 4 4 4 4 4 4 4 4 4 4 4 4 4 4
4 4 4 4 4 4 4 4 4 4 4 4 4 4 4 4 4 4 4 4 4 4 4 4 4 4 4 4 4 4 4 4
4 4 4 4 4 4 4 4 4 4 4 4 4 4 4 4 4 4 4 4 4 4 4 4 4 4 4 4 4 4 4 4
4 4 4 4 4 4 4 4 4 4 4 4 4 4 4 4 4 4 4 4 4 4 4 4 4 4 4 4 4 4 4 4
4 4 4 4 4 4 4 4 4 4 4 4 4 4 4 4 4 4 4 4 4 4 4 4 4 4 4 4 4 4 4 4

truly	hotel	behind	silent
focus	broken	predict	pretend
totem	decent	hijack	April
icon	student	chosen	cupid
began	token	even	robot
spoken	bacon	smoky	ivy

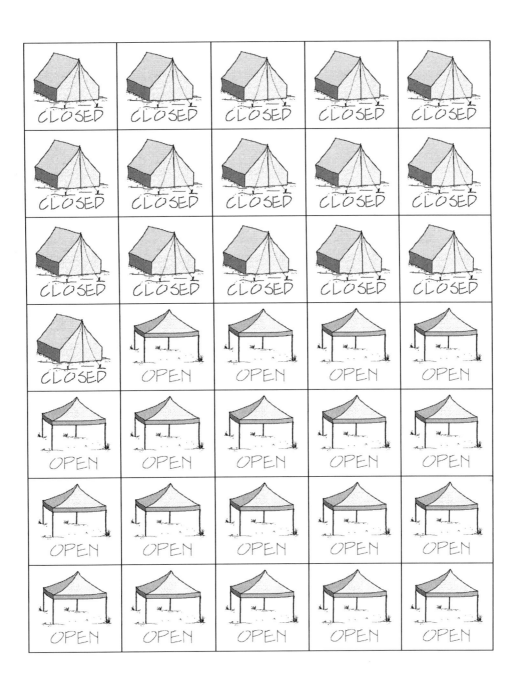

4 4 4 4 4 4 4 4 4 4 4 4 4 4 4 4 4 4 4 4 4 4 4 4 4 4 4 4 4 4 4 4
4 4 4 4 4 4 4 4 4 4 4 4 4 4 4 4 4 4 4 4 4 4 4 4 4 4 4 4 4 4 4 4
4 4 4 4 4 4 4 4 4 4 4 4 4 4 4 4 4 4 4 4 4 4 4 4 4 4 4 4 4 4 4 4
4 4 4 4 4 4 4 4 4 4 4 4 4 4 4 4 4 4 4 4 4 4 4 4 4 4 4 4 4 4 4 4
4 4 4 4 4 4 4 4 4 4 4 4 4 4 4 4 4 4 4 4 4 4 4 4 4 4 4 4 4 4 4 4
4 4 4 4 4 4 4 4 4 4 4 4 4 4 4 4 4 4 4 4 4 4 4 4 4 4 4 4 4 4 4 4
4 4 4 4 4 4 4 4 4 4 4 4 4 4 4 4 4 4 4 4 4 4 4 4 4 4 4 4 4 4 4 4
4 4 4 4 4 4 4 4 4 4 4 4 4 4 4 4 4 4 4 4 4 4 4 4 4 4 4 4 4 4 4 4
4 4 4 4 4 4 4 4 4 4 4 4 4 4 4 4 4 4 4 4 4 4 4 4 4 4 4 4 4 4 4 4
4 4 4 4 4 4 4 4 4 4 4 4 4 4 4 4 4 4 4 4 4 4 4 4 4 4 4 4 4 4 4 4
4 4 4 4 4 4 4 4 4 4 4 4 4 4 4 4 4 4 4 4 4 4 4 4 4 4 4 4 4 4 4 4
4 4 4 4 4 4 4 4 4 4 4 4 4 4 4 4 4 4 4 4 4 4 4 4 4 4 4 4 4 4 4 4
4 4 4 4 4 4 4 4 4 4 4 4 4 4 4 4 4 4 4 4 4 4 4 4 4 4 4 4 4 4 4 4
4 4 4 4 4 4 4 4 4 4 4 4 4 4 4 4 4 4 4 4 4 4 4 4 4 4 4 4 4 4 4 4
4 4 4 4 4 4 4 4 4 4 4 4 4 4 4 4 4 4 4 4 4 4 4 4 4 4 4 4 4 4 4 4
4 4 4 4 4 4 4 4 4 4 4 4 4 4 4 4 4 4 4 4 4 4 4 4 4 4 4 4 4 4 4 4
4 4 4 4 4 4 4 4 4 4 4 4 4 4 4 4 4 4 4 4 4 4 4 4 4 4 4 4 4 4 4 4
4 4 4 4 4 4 4 4 4 4 4 4 4 4 4 4 4 4 4 4 4 4 4 4 4 4 4 4 4 4 4 4
4 4 4 4 4 4 4 4 4 4 4 4 4 4 4 4 4 4 4 4 4 4 4 4 4 4 4 4 4 4 4 4
4 4 4 4 4 4 4 4 4 4 4 4 4 4 4 4 4 4 4 4 4 4 4 4 4 4 4 4 4 4 4 4
4 4 4 4 4 4 4 4 4 4 4 4 4 4 4 4 4 4 4 4 4 4 4 4 4 4 4 4 4 4 4 4
4 4 4 4 4 4 4 4 4 4 4 4 4 4 4 4 4 4 4 4 4 4 4 4 4 4 4 4 4 4 4 4
4 4 4 4 4 4 4 4 4 4 4 4 4 4 4 4 4 4 4 4 4 4 4 4 4 4 4 4 4 4 4 4
4 4 4 4 4 4 4 4 4 4 4 4 4 4 4 4 4 4 4 4 4 4 4 4 4 4 4 4 4 4 4 4
4 4 4 4 4 4 4 4 4 4 4 4 4 4 4 4 4 4 4 4 4 4 4 4 4 4 4 4 4 4 4 4
4 4 4 4 4 4 4 4 4 4 4 4 4 4 4 4 4 4 4 4 4 4 4 4 4 4 4 4 4 4 4 4
4 4 4 4 4 4 4 4 4 4 4 4 4 4 4 4 4 4 4 4 4 4 4 4 4 4 4 4 4 4 4 4
4 4 4 4 4 4 4 4 4 4 4 4 4 4 4 4 4 4 4 4 4 4 4 4 4 4 4 4 4 4 4 4
4 4 4 4 4 4 4 4 4 4 4 4 4 4 4 4 4 4 4 4 4 4 4 4 4 4 4 4 4 4 4 4
4 4 4 4 4 4 4 4 4 4 4 4 4 4 4 4 4 4 4 4 4 4 4 4 4 4 4 4 4 4 4 4
4 4 4 4 4 4 4 4 4 4 4 4 4 4 4 4 4 4 4 4 4 4 4 4 4 4 4 4 4 4 4 4
4 4 4 4 4 4 4 4 4 4 4 4 4 4 4 4 4 4 4 4 4 4 4 4 4 4 4 4 4 4 4 4
4 4 4 4 4 4 4 4 4 4 4 4 4 4 4 4 4 4 4 4 4 4 4 4 4 4 4 4 4 4 4 4

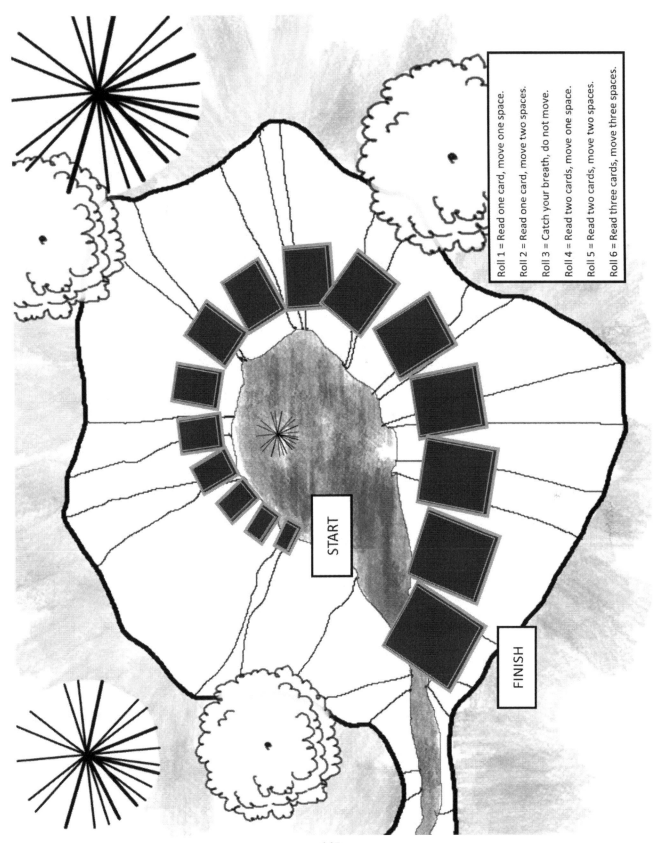

Roll 1 = Read one card, move one space.

Roll 2 = Read one card, move two spaces.

Roll 3 = Catch your breath, do not move.

Roll 4 = Read two cards, move one space.

Roll 5 = Read two cards, move two spaces.

Roll 6 = Read three cards, move three spaces.

START

FINISH

panic	expect	pesky	problem
hidden	tactic	sudden	almost
dizzy	stinky	frolic	classic
address	confess	compress	also
walnut	access	emboss	excess
obsess	across	campus	thesis

census	puppy	motto	guppy
hippo	kitty	shabby	rabbit
sunny	flabby	rubbish	daddy
choppy	snappy	patty	expo
foggy	squall	funny	sunny
summit	bunny	suffix	expend

5 5 5 5 5 5 5 5 5 5 5 5 5 5 5 5 5 5 5 5 5 5 5 5 5 5 5 5 5 5 5
5 5 5 5 5 5 5 5 5 5 5 5 5 5 5 5 5 5 5 5 5 5 5 5 5 5 5 5 5 5 5
5 5 5 5 5 5 5 5 5 5 5 5 5 5 5 5 5 5 5 5 5 5 5 5 5 5 5 5 5 5 5
5 5 5 5 5 5 5 5 5 5 5 5 5 5 5 5 5 5 5 5 5 5 5 5 5 5 5 5 5 5 5
5 5 5 5 5 5 5 5 5 5 5 5 5 5 5 5 5 5 5 5 5 5 5 5 5 5 5 5 5 5 5
5 5 5 5 5 5 5 5 5 5 5 5 5 5 5 5 5 5 5 5 5 5 5 5 5 5 5 5 5 5 5
5 5 5 5 5 5 5 5 5 5 5 5 5 5 5 5 5 5 5 5 5 5 5 5 5 5 5 5 5 5 5
5 5 5 5 5 5 5 5 5 5 5 5 5 5 5 5 5 5 5 5 5 5 5 5 5 5 5 5 5 5 5
5 5 5 5 5 5 5 5 5 5 5 5 5 5 5 5 5 5 5 5 5 5 5 5 5 5 5 5 5 5 5
5 5 5 5 5 5 5 5 5 5 5 5 5 5 5 5 5 5 5 5 5 5 5 5 5 5 5 5 5 5 5
5 5 5 5 5 5 5 5 5 5 5 5 5 5 5 5 5 5 5 5 5 5 5 5 5 5 5 5 5 5 5
5 5 5 5 5 5 5 5 5 5 5 5 5 5 5 5 5 5 5 5 5 5 5 5 5 5 5 5 5 5 5
5 5 5 5 5 5 5 5 5 5 5 5 5 5 5 5 5 5 5 5 5 5 5 5 5 5 5 5 5 5 5
5 5 5 5 5 5 5 5 5 5 5 5 5 5 5 5 5 5 5 5 5 5 5 5 5 5 5 5 5 5 5
5 5 5 5 5 5 5 5 5 5 5 5 5 5 5 5 5 5 5 5 5 5 5 5 5 5 5 5 5 5 5
5 5 5 5 5 5 5 5 5 5 5 5 5 5 5 5 5 5 5 5 5 5 5 5 5 5 5 5 5 5 5
5 5 5 5 5 5 5 5 5 5 5 5 5 5 5 5 5 5 5 5 5 5 5 5 5 5 5 5 5 5 5
5 5 5 5 5 5 5 5 5 5 5 5 5 5 5 5 5 5 5 5 5 5 5 5 5 5 5 5 5 5 5
5 5 5 5 5 5 5 5 5 5 5 5 5 5 5 5 5 5 5 5 5 5 5 5 5 5 5 5 5 5 5
5 5 5 5 5 5 5 5 5 5 5 5 5 5 5 5 5 5 5 5 5 5 5 5 5 5 5 5 5 5 5
5 5 5 5 5 5 5 5 5 5 5 5 5 5 5 5 5 5 5 5 5 5 5 5 5 5 5 5 5 5 5
5 5 5 5 5 5 5 5 5 5 5 5 5 5 5 5 5 5 5 5 5 5 5 5 5 5 5 5 5 5 5
5 5 5 5 5 5 5 5 5 5 5 5 5 5 5 5 5 5 5 5 5 5 5 5 5 5 5 5 5 5 5
5 5 5 5 5 5 5 5 5 5 5 5 5 5 5 5 5 5 5 5 5 5 5 5 5 5 5 5 5 5 5
5 5 5 5 5 5 5 5 5 5 5 5 5 5 5 5 5 5 5 5 5 5 5 5 5 5 5 5 5 5 5
5 5 5 5 5 5 5 5 5 5 5 5 5 5 5 5 5 5 5 5 5 5 5 5 5 5 5 5 5 5 5
5 5 5 5 5 5 5 5 5 5 5 5 5 5 5 5 5 5 5 5 5 5 5 5 5 5 5 5 5 5 5
5 5 5 5 5 5 5 5 5 5 5 5 5 5 5 5 5 5 5 5 5 5 5 5 5 5 5 5 5 5 5
5 5 5 5 5 5 5 5 5 5 5 5 5 5 5 5 5 5 5 5 5 5 5 5 5 5 5 5 5 5 5
5 5 5 5 5 5 5 5 5 5 5 5 5 5 5 5 5 5 5 5 5 5 5 5 5 5 5 5 5 5 5
5 5 5 5 5 5 5 5 5 5 5 5 5 5 5 5 5 5 5 5 5 5 5 5 5 5 5 5 5 5 5
5 5 5 5 5 5 5 5 5 5 5 5 5 5 5 5 5 5 5 5 5 5 5 5 5 5 5 5 5 5 5

Board #1

Board #2

Board #3

Board #4

Board #5

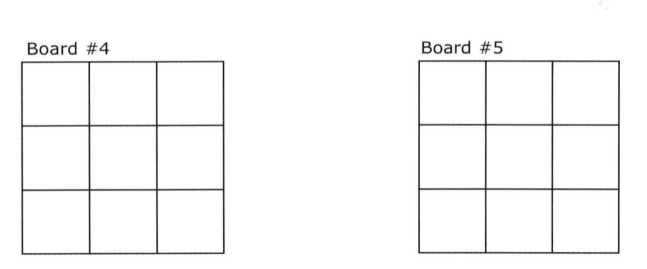

salad	human	Cuban	bottom
slogan	vegan	lemon	gallon
venom	atom	bacon	dragon
piston	wagon	bison	vital
petal	label	idol	evil
pupil	camel	dental	flannel

6 6 6 6 6 6 6 6 6 6 6 6 6 6 6 6 6 6 6 6 6 6 6 6 6 6 6 6 6 6 6 6 6 6 6 6
6 6 6 6 6 6 6 6 6 6 6 6 6 6 6 6 6 6 6 6 6 6 6 6 6 6 6 6 6 6 6 6 6 6 6 6
6 6 6 6 6 6 6 6 6 6 6 6 6 6 6 6 6 6 6 6 6 6 6 6 6 6 6 6 6 6 6 6 6 6 6 6
6 6 6 6 6 6 6 6 6 6 6 6 6 6 6 6 6 6 6 6 6 6 6 6 6 6 6 6 6 6 6 6 6 6 6 6
6 6 6 6 6 6 6 6 6 6 6 6 6 6 6 6 6 6 6 6 6 6 6 6 6 6 6 6 6 6 6 6 6 6 6 6
6 6 6 6 6 6 6 6 6 6 6 6 6 6 6 6 6 6 6 6 6 6 6 6 6 6 6 6 6 6 6 6 6 6 6 6
6 6 6 6 6 6 6 6 6 6 6 6 6 6 6 6 6 6 6 6 6 6 6 6 6 6 6 6 6 6 6 6 6 6 6 6
6 6 6 6 6 6 6 6 6 6 6 6 6 6 6 6 6 6 6 6 6 6 6 6 6 6 6 6 6 6 6 6 6 6 6 6
6 6 6 6 6 6 6 6 6 6 6 6 6 6 6 6 6 6 6 6 6 6 6 6 6 6 6 6 6 6 6 6 6 6 6 6
6 6 6 6 6 6 6 6 6 6 6 6 6 6 6 6 6 6 6 6 6 6 6 6 6 6 6 6 6 6 6 6 6 6 6 6
6 6 6 6 6 6 6 6 6 6 6 6 6 6 6 6 6 6 6 6 6 6 6 6 6 6 6 6 6 6 6 6 6 6 6 6
6 6 6 6 6 6 6 6 6 6 6 6 6 6 6 6 6 6 6 6 6 6 6 6 6 6 6 6 6 6 6 6 6 6 6 6
6 6 6 6 6 6 6 6 6 6 6 6 6 6 6 6 6 6 6 6 6 6 6 6 6 6 6 6 6 6 6 6 6 6 6 6
6 6 6 6 6 6 6 6 6 6 6 6 6 6 6 6 6 6 6 6 6 6 6 6 6 6 6 6 6 6 6 6 6 6 6 6
6 6 6 6 6 6 6 6 6 6 6 6 6 6 6 6 6 6 6 6 6 6 6 6 6 6 6 6 6 6 6 6 6 6 6 6
6 6 6 6 6 6 6 6 6 6 6 6 6 6 6 6 6 6 6 6 6 6 6 6 6 6 6 6 6 6 6 6 6 6 6 6
6 6 6 6 6 6 6 6 6 6 6 6 6 6 6 6 6 6 6 6 6 6 6 6 6 6 6 6 6 6 6 6 6 6 6 6
6 6 6 6 6 6 6 6 6 6 6 6 6 6 6 6 6 6 6 6 6 6 6 6 6 6 6 6 6 6 6 6 6 6 6 6
6 6 6 6 6 6 6 6 6 6 6 6 6 6 6 6 6 6 6 6 6 6 6 6 6 6 6 6 6 6 6 6 6 6 6 6
6 6 6 6 6 6 6 6 6 6 6 6 6 6 6 6 6 6 6 6 6 6 6 6 6 6 6 6 6 6 6 6 6 6 6 6
6 6 6 6 6 6 6 6 6 6 6 6 6 6 6 6 6 6 6 6 6 6 6 6 6 6 6 6 6 6 6 6 6 6 6 6
6 6 6 6 6 6 6 6 6 6 6 6 6 6 6 6 6 6 6 6 6 6 6 6 6 6 6 6 6 6 6 6 6 6 6 6
6 6 6 6 6 6 6 6 6 6 6 6 6 6 6 6 6 6 6 6 6 6 6 6 6 6 6 6 6 6 6 6 6 6 6 6
6 6 6 6 6 6 6 6 6 6 6 6 6 6 6 6 6 6 6 6 6 6 6 6 6 6 6 6 6 6 6 6 6 6 6 6
6 6 6 6 6 6 6 6 6 6 6 6 6 6 6 6 6 6 6 6 6 6 6 6 6 6 6 6 6 6 6 6 6 6 6 6
6 6 6 6 6 6 6 6 6 6 6 6 6 6 6 6 6 6 6 6 6 6 6 6 6 6 6 6 6 6 6 6 6 6 6 6
6 6 6 6 6 6 6 6 6 6 6 6 6 6 6 6 6 6 6 6 6 6 6 6 6 6 6 6 6 6 6 6 6 6 6 6
6 6 6 6 6 6 6 6 6 6 6 6 6 6 6 6 6 6 6 6 6 6 6 6 6 6 6 6 6 6 6 6 6 6 6 6
6 6 6 6 6 6 6 6 6 6 6 6 6 6 6 6 6 6 6 6 6 6 6 6 6 6 6 6 6 6 6 6 6 6 6 6
6 6 6 6 6 6 6 6 6 6 6 6 6 6 6 6 6 6 6 6 6 6 6 6 6 6 6 6 6 6 6 6 6 6 6 6
6 6 6 6 6 6 6 6 6 6 6 6 6 6 6 6 6 6 6 6 6 6 6 6 6 6 6 6 6 6 6 6 6 6 6 6
6 6 6 6 6 6 6 6 6 6 6 6 6 6 6 6 6 6 6 6 6 6 6 6 6 6 6 6 6 6 6 6 6 6 6 6
6 6 6 6 6 6 6 6 6 6 6 6 6 6 6 6 6 6 6 6 6 6 6 6 6 6 6 6 6 6 6 6 6 6 6 6

tunnel	metal	hazel	local
pedal	spiral	total	travel
cancel	sandal	tidal	shock
happy	recess	absent	toxic
began	modest	find	gold
nugget	remind	messy	baby

6 6 6 6 6 6 6 6 6 6 6 6 6 6 6 6 6 6 6 6 6 6 6 6 6 6 6 6 6 6
6 6 6 6 6 6 6 6 6 6 6 6 6 6 6 6 6 6 6 6 6 6 6 6 6 6 6 6 6 6
6 6 6 6 6 6 6 6 6 6 6 6 6 6 6 6 6 6 6 6 6 6 6 6 6 6 6 6 6 6
6 6 6 6 6 6 6 6 6 6 6 6 6 6 6 6 6 6 6 6 6 6 6 6 6 6 6 6 6 6
6 6 6 6 6 6 6 6 6 6 6 6 6 6 6 6 6 6 6 6 6 6 6 6 6 6 6 6 6 6
6 6 6 6 6 6 6 6 6 6 6 6 6 6 6 6 6 6 6 6 6 6 6 6 6 6 6 6 6 6
6 6 6 6 6 6 6 6 6 6 6 6 6 6 6 6 6 6 6 6 6 6 6 6 6 6 6 6 6 6
6 6 6 6 6 6 6 6 6 6 6 6 6 6 6 6 6 6 6 6 6 6 6 6 6 6 6 6 6 6
6 6 6 6 6 6 6 6 6 6 6 6 6 6 6 6 6 6 6 6 6 6 6 6 6 6 6 6 6 6
6 6 6 6 6 6 6 6 6 6 6 6 6 6 6 6 6 6 6 6 6 6 6 6 6 6 6 6 6 6
6 6 6 6 6 6 6 6 6 6 6 6 6 6 6 6 6 6 6 6 6 6 6 6 6 6 6 6 6 6
6 6 6 6 6 6 6 6 6 6 6 6 6 6 6 6 6 6 6 6 6 6 6 6 6 6 6 6 6 6
6 6 6 6 6 6 6 6 6 6 6 6 6 6 6 6 6 6 6 6 6 6 6 6 6 6 6 6 6 6
6 6 6 6 6 6 6 6 6 6 6 6 6 6 6 6 6 6 6 6 6 6 6 6 6 6 6 6 6 6
6 6 6 6 6 6 6 6 6 6 6 6 6 6 6 6 6 6 6 6 6 6 6 6 6 6 6 6 6 6
6 6 6 6 6 6 6 6 6 6 6 6 6 6 6 6 6 6 6 6 6 6 6 6 6 6 6 6 6 6
6 6 6 6 6 6 6 6 6 6 6 6 6 6 6 6 6 6 6 6 6 6 6 6 6 6 6 6 6 6
6 6 6 6 6 6 6 6 6 6 6 6 6 6 6 6 6 6 6 6 6 6 6 6 6 6 6 6 6 6
6 6 6 6 6 6 6 6 6 6 6 6 6 6 6 6 6 6 6 6 6 6 6 6 6 6 6 6 6 6
6 6 6 6 6 6 6 6 6 6 6 6 6 6 6 6 6 6 6 6 6 6 6 6 6 6 6 6 6 6
6 6 6 6 6 6 6 6 6 6 6 6 6 6 6 6 6 6 6 6 6 6 6 6 6 6 6 6 6 6
6 6 6 6 6 6 6 6 6 6 6 6 6 6 6 6 6 6 6 6 6 6 6 6 6 6 6 6 6 6
6 6 6 6 6 6 6 6 6 6 6 6 6 6 6 6 6 6 6 6 6 6 6 6 6 6 6 6 6 6
6 6 6 6 6 6 6 6 6 6 6 6 6 6 6 6 6 6 6 6 6 6 6 6 6 6 6 6 6 6
6 6 6 6 6 6 6 6 6 6 6 6 6 6 6 6 6 6 6 6 6 6 6 6 6 6 6 6 6 6
6 6 6 6 6 6 6 6 6 6 6 6 6 6 6 6 6 6 6 6 6 6 6 6 6 6 6 6 6 6
6 6 6 6 6 6 6 6 6 6 6 6 6 6 6 6 6 6 6 6 6 6 6 6 6 6 6 6 6 6
6 6 6 6 6 6 6 6 6 6 6 6 6 6 6 6 6 6 6 6 6 6 6 6 6 6 6 6 6 6
6 6 6 6 6 6 6 6 6 6 6 6 6 6 6 6 6 6 6 6 6 6 6 6 6 6 6 6 6 6
6 6 6 6 6 6 6 6 6 6 6 6 6 6 6 6 6 6 6 6 6 6 6 6 6 6 6 6 6 6
6 6 6 6 6 6 6 6 6 6 6 6 6 6 6 6 6 6 6 6 6 6 6 6 6 6 6 6 6 6
6 6 6 6 6 6 6 6 6 6 6 6 6 6 6 6 6 6 6 6 6 6 6 6 6 6 6 6 6 6
6 6 6 6 6 6 6 6 6 6 6 6 6 6 6 6 6 6 6 6 6 6 6 6 6 6 6 6 6 6

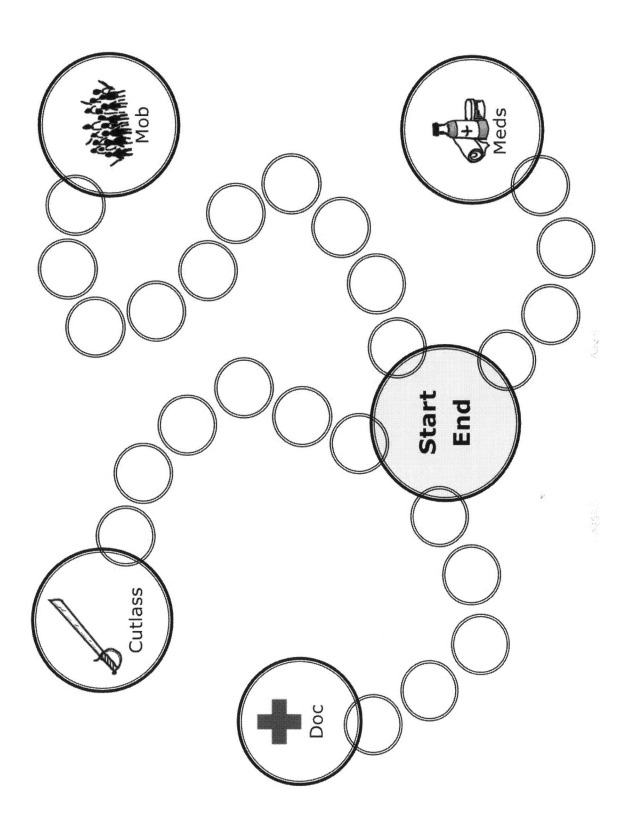

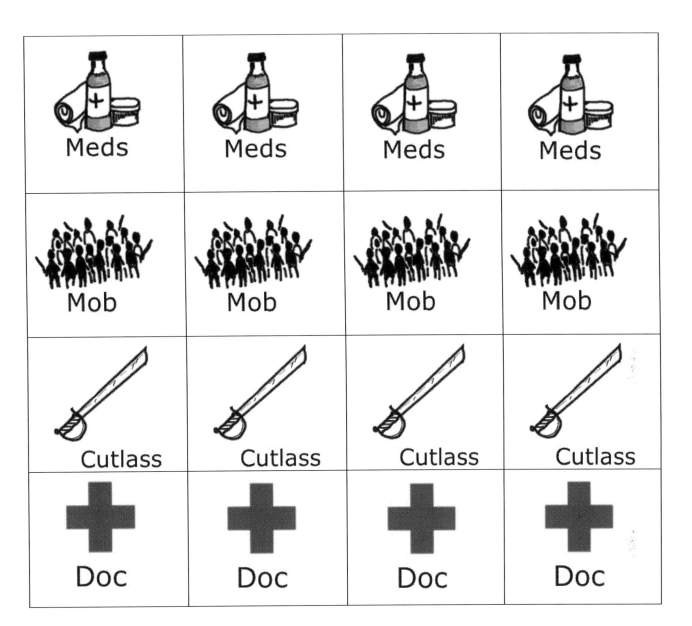

7 7 7 7 7 7 7 7 7 7 7 7 7 7 7 7 7 7 7 7 7 7 7 7 7 7 7 7 7
7 7 7 7 7 7 7 7 7 7 7 7 7 7 7 7 7 7 7 7 7 7 7 7 7 7 7 7 7
7 7 7 7 7 7 7 7 7 7 7 7 7 7 7 7 7 7 7 7 7 7 7 7 7 7 7 7 7
7 7 7 7 7 7 7 7 7 7 7 7 7 7 7 7 7 7 7 7 7 7 7 7 7 7 7 7 7
7 7 7 7 7 7 7 7 7 7 7 7 7 7 7 7 7 7 7 7 7 7 7 7 7 7 7 7 7
7 7 7 7 7 7 7 7 7 7 7 7 7 7 7 7 7 7 7 7 7 7 7 7 7 7 7 7 7
7 7 7 7 7 7 7 7 7 7 7 7 7 7 7 7 7 7 7 7 7 7 7 7 7 7 7 7 7
7 7 7 7 7 7 7 7 7 7 7 7 7 7 7 7 7 7 7 7 7 7 7 7 7 7 7 7 7
7 7 7 7 7 7 7 7 7 7 7 7 7 7 7 7 7 7 7 7 7 7 7 7 7 7 7 7 7
7 7 7 7 7 7 7 7 7 7 7 7 7 7 7 7 7 7 7 7 7 7 7 7 7 7 7 7 7
7 7 7 7 7 7 7 7 7 7 7 7 7 7 7 7 7 7 7 7 7 7 7 7 7 7 7 7 7
7 7 7 7 7 7 7 7 7 7 7 7 7 7 7 7 7 7 7 7 7 7 7 7 7 7 7 7 7
7 7 7 7 7 7 7 7 7 7 7 7 7 7 7 7 7 7 7 7 7 7 7 7 7 7 7 7 7
7 7 7 7 7 7 7 7 7 7 7 7 7 7 7 7 7 7 7 7 7 7 7 7 7 7 7 7 7
7 7 7 7 7 7 7 7 7 7 7 7 7 7 7 7 7 7 7 7 7 7 7 7 7 7 7 7 7
7 7 7 7 7 7 7 7 7 7 7 7 7 7 7 7 7 7 7 7 7 7 7 7 7 7 7 7 7
7 7 7 7 7 7 7 7 7 7 7 7 7 7 7 7 7 7 7 7 7 7 7 7 7 7 7 7 7
7 7 7 7 7 7 7 7 7 7 7 7 7 7 7 7 7 7 7 7 7 7 7 7 7 7 7 7 7
7 7 7 7 7 7 7 7 7 7 7 7 7 7 7 7 7 7 7 7 7 7 7 7 7 7 7 7 7
7 7 7 7 7 7 7 7 7 7 7 7 7 7 7 7 7 7 7 7 7 7 7 7 7 7 7 7 7
7 7 7 7 7 7 7 7 7 7 7 7 7 7 7 7 7 7 7 7 7 7 7 7 7 7 7 7 7
7 7 7 7 7 7 7 7 7 7 7 7 7 7 7 7 7 7 7 7 7 7 7 7 7 7 7 7 7
7 7 7 7 7 7 7 7 7 7 7 7 7 7 7 7 7 7 7 7 7 7 7 7 7 7 7 7 7
7 7 7 7 7 7 7 7 7 7 7 7 7 7 7 7 7 7 7 7 7 7 7 7 7 7 7 7 7
7 7 7 7 7 7 7 7 7 7 7 7 7 7 7 7 7 7 7 7 7 7 7 7 7 7 7 7 7
7 7 7 7 7 7 7 7 7 7 7 7 7 7 7 7 7 7 7 7 7 7 7 7 7 7 7 7 7
7 7 7 7 7 7 7 7 7 7 7 7 7 7 7 7 7 7 7 7 7 7 7 7 7 7 7 7 7
7 7 7 7 7 7 7 7 7 7 7 7 7 7 7 7 7 7 7 7 7 7 7 7 7 7 7 7 7
7 7 7 7 7 7 7 7 7 7 7 7 7 7 7 7 7 7 7 7 7 7 7 7 7 7 7 7 7
7 7 7 7 7 7 7 7 7 7 7 7 7 7 7 7 7 7 7 7 7 7 7 7 7 7 7 7 7

fulcrum	contract	instinct	express
complex	conflict	grassland	subtract
distress	compress	ethnic	contrast
hundred	control	checklist	address
instant	saffron	extract	hungry
handbag	children	congress	impress

bathtub	dishrag	softball	address
constant	quicksand	sundress	sunblock
sunspot	goldfish	postman	kitchen
backpack	plankton	tantrum	district
softball	anthill	entry	lipstick
central	fastball	hopscotch	duckling

1	2	3	4	5	6
7	8	9	10	11	12
13	14	15	16	17	18
19	20	21	22	23	24

abstract	instruct	construct
R. L. Nox's Army move to #21	R. L. Nox's Army move to #22	R. L. Nox's Army move to #5
Dragon move 3	Dragon move 2	Dragon move 1
Player Move 1	Player Move 2	Player Move 1
transcript	**subscript**	**obstruct**
R. L. Nox's Army move to #1	R. L. Nox's Army move to #24	R. L. Nox's Army move to #2
Dragon move 1		
Player Move 2	Player Move 2	Player Move 3
constrict	**dishcloth**	**munchkin**
R. L. Nox's Army move to #3	R. L. Nox's Army move to #4	R. L. Nox's Army move to #23
Player Move 1	Player Move 1	Player Move 1
backstretch	**backhand**	**backsplash**
R. L. Nox's Army move to #6	R. L. Nox's Army move to #7	R. L. Nox's Army move to #8
Player Move 2	Player Move 2	Player Move 3

8 8 8 8 8 8 8 8 8 8 8 8 8 8 8 8 8 8 8 8 8 8 8 8 8 8 8 8 8 8 8 8 8 8
8 8 8 8 8 8 8 8 8 8 8 8 8 8 8 8 8 8 8 8 8 8 8 8 8 8 8 8 8 8 8 8 8 8
8 8 8 8 8 8 8 8 8 8 8 8 8 8 8 8 8 8 8 8 8 8 8 8 8 8 8 8 8 8 8 8 8 8
8 8 8 8 8 8 8 8 8 8 8 8 8 8 8 8 8 8 8 8 8 8 8 8 8 8 8 8 8 8 8 8 8 8
8 8 8 8 8 8 8 8 8 8 8 8 8 8 8 8 8 8 8 8 8 8 8 8 8 8 8 8 8 8 8 8 8 8
8 8 8 8 8 8 8 8 8 8 8 8 8 8 8 8 8 8 8 8 8 8 8 8 8 8 8 8 8 8 8 8 8 8
8 8 8 8 8 8 8 8 8 8 8 8 8 8 8 8 8 8 8 8 8 8 8 8 8 8 8 8 8 8 8 8 8 8
8 8 8 8 8 8 8 8 8 8 8 8 8 8 8 8 8 8 8 8 8 8 8 8 8 8 8 8 8 8 8 8 8 8
8 8 8 8 8 8 8 8 8 8 8 8 8 8 8 8 8 8 8 8 8 8 8 8 8 8 8 8 8 8 8 8 8 8
8 8 8 8 8 8 8 8 8 8 8 8 8 8 8 8 8 8 8 8 8 8 8 8 8 8 8 8 8 8 8 8 8 8
8 8 8 8 8 8 8 8 8 8 8 8 8 8 8 8 8 8 8 8 8 8 8 8 8 8 8 8 8 8 8 8 8 8
8 8 8 8 8 8 8 8 8 8 8 8 8 8 8 8 8 8 8 8 8 8 8 8 8 8 8 8 8 8 8 8 8 8
8 8 8 8 8 8 8 8 8 8 8 8 8 8 8 8 8 8 8 8 8 8 8 8 8 8 8 8 8 8 8 8 8 8
8 8 8 8 8 8 8 8 8 8 8 8 8 8 8 8 8 8 8 8 8 8 8 8 8 8 8 8 8 8 8 8 8 8
8 8 8 8 8 8 8 8 8 8 8 8 8 8 8 8 8 8 8 8 8 8 8 8 8 8 8 8 8 8 8 8 8 8
8 8 8 8 8 8 8 8 8 8 8 8 8 8 8 8 8 8 8 8 8 8 8 8 8 8 8 8 8 8 8 8 8 8
8 8 8 8 8 8 8 8 8 8 8 8 8 8 8 8 8 8 8 8 8 8 8 8 8 8 8 8 8 8 8 8 8 8
8 8 8 8 8 8 8 8 8 8 8 8 8 8 8 8 8 8 8 8 8 8 8 8 8 8 8 8 8 8 8 8 8 8
8 8 8 8 8 8 8 8 8 8 8 8 8 8 8 8 8 8 8 8 8 8 8 8 8 8 8 8 8 8 8 8 8 8
8 8 8 8 8 8 8 8 8 8 8 8 8 8 8 8 8 8 8 8 8 8 8 8 8 8 8 8 8 8 8 8 8 8
8 8 8 8 8 8 8 8 8 8 8 8 8 8 8 8 8 8 8 8 8 8 8 8 8 8 8 8 8 8 8 8 8 8
8 8 8 8 8 8 8 8 8 8 8 8 8 8 8 8 8 8 8 8 8 8 8 8 8 8 8 8 8 8 8 8 8 8
8 8 8 8 8 8 8 8 8 8 8 8 8 8 8 8 8 8 8 8 8 8 8 8 8 8 8 8 8 8 8 8 8 8
8 8 8 8 8 8 8 8 8 8 8 8 8 8 8 8 8 8 8 8 8 8 8 8 8 8 8 8 8 8 8 8 8 8
8 8 8 8 8 8 8 8 8 8 8 8 8 8 8 8 8 8 8 8 8 8 8 8 8 8 8 8 8 8 8 8 8 8
8 8 8 8 8 8 8 8 8 8 8 8 8 8 8 8 8 8 8 8 8 8 8 8 8 8 8 8 8 8 8 8 8 8
8 8 8 8 8 8 8 8 8 8 8 8 8 8 8 8 8 8 8 8 8 8 8 8 8 8 8 8 8 8 8 8 8 8
8 8 8 8 8 8 8 8 8 8 8 8 8 8 8 8 8 8 8 8 8 8 8 8 8 8 8 8 8 8 8 8 8 8
8 8 8 8 8 8 8 8 8 8 8 8 8 8 8 8 8 8 8 8 8 8 8 8 8 8 8 8 8 8 8 8 8 8
8 8 8 8 8 8 8 8 8 8 8 8 8 8 8 8 8 8 8 8 8 8 8 8 8 8 8 8 8 8 8 8 8 8

backstitch	**bedspring**	**withstand**
R. L. Nox's Army move to #9	R. L. Nox's Army move to #10	R. L. Nox's Army move to #11
Player Move 1	Player Move 1	Player Move 2
standstill	**matchbox**	**handstand**
R. L. Nox's Army move to #12	R. L. Nox's Army move to #13	R. L. Nox's Army move to #14
Player Move 3	Player Move 1	Player Move 1
standoff	**lunchbox**	**grandchild**
R. L. Nox's Army move to #15	R. L. Nox's Army move to #16	R. L. Nox's Army move to #17
Player Move 2	Player Move 3	Player Move 1
locksmith	**bunchgrass**	**benchtop**
R. L. Nox's Army move to #18	R. L. Nox's Army move to #19	R. L. Nox's Army move to #20
Player Move 2	Player Move 2	Player Move 3

8 8 8 8 8 8 8 8 8 8 8 8 8 8 8 8 8 8 8 8 8 8 8 8 8 8 8 8 8 8 8 8 8 8 8 8 8 8 8 8
8 8 8 8 8 8 8 8 8 8 8 8 8 8 8 8 8 8 8 8 8 8 8 8 8 8 8 8 8 8 8 8 8 8 8 8 8 8 8 8
8 8 8 8 8 8 8 8 8 8 8 8 8 8 8 8 8 8 8 8 8 8 8 8 8 8 8 8 8 8 8 8 8 8 8 8 8 8 8 8
8 8 8 8 8 8 8 8 8 8 8 8 8 8 8 8 8 8 8 8 8 8 8 8 8 8 8 8 8 8 8 8 8 8 8 8 8 8 8 8
8 8 8 8 8 8 8 8 8 8 8 8 8 8 8 8 8 8 8 8 8 8 8 8 8 8 8 8 8 8 8 8 8 8 8 8 8 8 8 8
8 8 8 8 8 8 8 8 8 8 8 8 8 8 8 8 8 8 8 8 8 8 8 8 8 8 8 8 8 8 8 8 8 8 8 8 8 8 8 8
8 8 8 8 8 8 8 8 8 8 8 8 8 8 8 8 8 8 8 8 8 8 8 8 8 8 8 8 8 8 8 8 8 8 8 8 8 8 8 8
8 8 8 8 8 8 8 8 8 8 8 8 8 8 8 8 8 8 8 8 8 8 8 8 8 8 8 8 8 8 8 8 8 8 8 8 8 8 8 8
8 8 8 8 8 8 8 8 8 8 8 8 8 8 8 8 8 8 8 8 8 8 8 8 8 8 8 8 8 8 8 8 8 8 8 8 8 8 8 8
8 8 8 8 8 8 8 8 8 8 8 8 8 8 8 8 8 8 8 8 8 8 8 8 8 8 8 8 8 8 8 8 8 8 8 8 8 8 8 8
8 8 8 8 8 8 8 8 8 8 8 8 8 8 8 8 8 8 8 8 8 8 8 8 8 8 8 8 8 8 8 8 8 8 8 8 8 8 8 8
8 8 8 8 8 8 8 8 8 8 8 8 8 8 8 8 8 8 8 8 8 8 8 8 8 8 8 8 8 8 8 8 8 8 8 8 8 8 8 8
8 8 8 8 8 8 8 8 8 8 8 8 8 8 8 8 8 8 8 8 8 8 8 8 8 8 8 8 8 8 8 8 8 8 8 8 8 8 8 8
8 8 8 8 8 8 8 8 8 8 8 8 8 8 8 8 8 8 8 8 8 8 8 8 8 8 8 8 8 8 8 8 8 8 8 8 8 8 8 8
8 8 8 8 8 8 8 8 8 8 8 8 8 8 8 8 8 8 8 8 8 8 8 8 8 8 8 8 8 8 8 8 8 8 8 8 8 8 8 8
8 8 8 8 8 8 8 8 8 8 8 8 8 8 8 8 8 8 8 8 8 8 8 8 8 8 8 8 8 8 8 8 8 8 8 8 8 8 8 8
8 8 8 8 8 8 8 8 8 8 8 8 8 8 8 8 8 8 8 8 8 8 8 8 8 8 8 8 8 8 8 8 8 8 8 8 8 8 8 8
8 8 8 8 8 8 8 8 8 8 8 8 8 8 8 8 8 8 8 8 8 8 8 8 8 8 8 8 8 8 8 8 8 8 8 8 8 8 8 8
8 8 8 8 8 8 8 8 8 8 8 8 8 8 8 8 8 8 8 8 8 8 8 8 8 8 8 8 8 8 8 8 8 8 8 8 8 8 8 8
8 8 8 8 8 8 8 8 8 8 8 8 8 8 8 8 8 8 8 8 8 8 8 8 8 8 8 8 8 8 8 8 8 8 8 8 8 8 8 8
8 8 8 8 8 8 8 8 8 8 8 8 8 8 8 8 8 8 8 8 8 8 8 8 8 8 8 8 8 8 8 8 8 8 8 8 8 8 8 8
8 8 8 8 8 8 8 8 8 8 8 8 8 8 8 8 8 8 8 8 8 8 8 8 8 8 8 8 8 8 8 8 8 8 8 8 8 8 8 8
8 8 8 8 8 8 8 8 8 8 8 8 8 8 8 8 8 8 8 8 8 8 8 8 8 8 8 8 8 8 8 8 8 8 8 8 8 8 8 8
8 8 8 8 8 8 8 8 8 8 8 8 8 8 8 8 8 8 8 8 8 8 8 8 8 8 8 8 8 8 8 8 8 8 8 8 8 8 8 8
8 8 8 8 8 8 8 8 8 8 8 8 8 8 8 8 8 8 8 8 8 8 8 8 8 8 8 8 8 8 8 8 8 8 8 8 8 8 8 8
8 8 8 8 8 8 8 8 8 8 8 8 8 8 8 8 8 8 8 8 8 8 8 8 8 8 8 8 8 8 8 8 8 8 8 8 8 8 8 8
8 8 8 8 8 8 8 8 8 8 8 8 8 8 8 8 8 8 8 8 8 8 8 8 8 8 8 8 8 8 8 8 8 8 8 8 8 8 8 8
8 8 8 8 8 8 8 8 8 8 8 8 8 8 8 8 8 8 8 8 8 8 8 8 8 8 8 8 8 8 8 8 8 8 8 8 8 8 8 8
8 8 8 8 8 8 8 8 8 8 8 8 8 8 8 8 8 8 8 8 8 8 8 8 8 8 8 8 8 8 8 8 8 8 8 8 8 8 8 8
8 8 8 8 8 8 8 8 8 8 8 8 8 8 8 8 8 8 8 8 8 8 8 8 8 8 8 8 8 8 8 8 8 8 8 8 8 8 8 8
8 8 8 8 8 8 8 8 8 8 8 8 8 8 8 8 8 8 8 8 8 8 8 8 8 8 8 8 8 8 8 8 8 8 8 8 8 8 8 8
8 8 8 8 8 8 8 8 8 8 8 8 8 8 8 8 8 8 8 8 8 8 8 8 8 8 8 8 8 8 8 8 8 8 8 8 8 8 8 8
8 8 8 8 8 8 8 8 8 8 8 8 8 8 8 8 8 8 8 8 8 8 8 8 8 8 8 8 8 8 8 8 8 8 8 8 8 8 8 8

de	pen	dent	po
ten	cy	dim	in
ish	ap	pre	hend
vol	can	ic	al
man	ac	in	vest
ment	re	pub	lic
dem	o	crat	la

9 9 9 9 9 9 9 9 9 9 9 9 9 9 9 9 9 9 9 9 9 9 9 9 9 9 9 9 9 9 9 9 9 9 9 9 9
9 9 9 9 9 9 9 9 9 9 9 9 9 9 9 9 9 9 9 9 9 9 9 9 9 9 9 9 9 9 9 9 9 9 9 9 9
9 9 9 9 9 9 9 9 9 9 9 9 9 9 9 9 9 9 9 9 9 9 9 9 9 9 9 9 9 9 9 9 9 9 9 9 9
9 9 9 9 9 9 9 9 9 9 9 9 9 9 9 9 9 9 9 9 9 9 9 9 9 9 9 9 9 9 9 9 9 9 9 9 9
9 9 9 9 9 9 9 9 9 9 9 9 9 9 9 9 9 9 9 9 9 9 9 9 9 9 9 9 9 9 9 9 9 9 9 9 9
9 9 9 9 9 9 9 9 9 9 9 9 9 9 9 9 9 9 9 9 9 9 9 9 9 9 9 9 9 9 9 9 9 9 9 9 9
9 9 9 9 9 9 9 9 9 9 9 9 9 9 9 9 9 9 9 9 9 9 9 9 9 9 9 9 9 9 9 9 9 9 9 9 9
9 9 9 9 9 9 9 9 9 9 9 9 9 9 9 9 9 9 9 9 9 9 9 9 9 9 9 9 9 9 9 9 9 9 9 9 9
9 9 9 9 9 9 9 9 9 9 9 9 9 9 9 9 9 9 9 9 9 9 9 9 9 9 9 9 9 9 9 9 9 9 9 9 9
9 9 9 9 9 9 9 9 9 9 9 9 9 9 9 9 9 9 9 9 9 9 9 9 9 9 9 9 9 9 9 9 9 9 9 9 9
9 9 9 9 9 9 9 9 9 9 9 9 9 9 9 9 9 9 9 9 9 9 9 9 9 9 9 9 9 9 9 9 9 9 9 9 9
9 9 9 9 9 9 9 9 9 9 9 9 9 9 9 9 9 9 9 9 9 9 9 9 9 9 9 9 9 9 9 9 9 9 9 9 9
9 9 9 9 9 9 9 9 9 9 9 9 9 9 9 9 9 9 9 9 9 9 9 9 9 9 9 9 9 9 9 9 9 9 9 9 9
9 9 9 9 9 9 9 9 9 9 9 9 9 9 9 9 9 9 9 9 9 9 9 9 9 9 9 9 9 9 9 9 9 9 9 9 9
9 9 9 9 9 9 9 9 9 9 9 9 9 9 9 9 9 9 9 9 9 9 9 9 9 9 9 9 9 9 9 9 9 9 9 9 9
9 9 9 9 9 9 9 9 9 9 9 9 9 9 9 9 9 9 9 9 9 9 9 9 9 9 9 9 9 9 9 9 9 9 9 9 9
9 9 9 9 9 9 9 9 9 9 9 9 9 9 9 9 9 9 9 9 9 9 9 9 9 9 9 9 9 9 9 9 9 9 9 9 9
9 9 9 9 9 9 9 9 9 9 9 9 9 9 9 9 9 9 9 9 9 9 9 9 9 9 9 9 9 9 9 9 9 9 9 9 9
9 9 9 9 9 9 9 9 9 9 9 9 9 9 9 9 9 9 9 9 9 9 9 9 9 9 9 9 9 9 9 9 9 9 9 9 9
9 9 9 9 9 9 9 9 9 9 9 9 9 9 9 9 9 9 9 9 9 9 9 9 9 9 9 9 9 9 9 9 9 9 9 9 9
9 9 9 9 9 9 9 9 9 9 9 9 9 9 9 9 9 9 9 9 9 9 9 9 9 9 9 9 9 9 9 9 9 9 9 9 9
9 9 9 9 9 9 9 9 9 9 9 9 9 9 9 9 9 9 9 9 9 9 9 9 9 9 9 9 9 9 9 9 9 9 9 9 9
9 9 9 9 9 9 9 9 9 9 9 9 9 9 9 9 9 9 9 9 9 9 9 9 9 9 9 9 9 9 9 9 9 9 9 9 9
9 9 9 9 9 9 9 9 9 9 9 9 9 9 9 9 9 9 9 9 9 9 9 9 9 9 9 9 9 9 9 9 9 9 9 9 9
9 9 9 9 9 9 9 9 9 9 9 9 9 9 9 9 9 9 9 9 9 9 9 9 9 9 9 9 9 9 9 9 9 9 9 9 9
9 9 9 9 9 9 9 9 9 9 9 9 9 9 9 9 9 9 9 9 9 9 9 9 9 9 9 9 9 9 9 9 9 9 9 9 9
9 9 9 9 9 9 9 9 9 9 9 9 9 9 9 9 9 9 9 9 9 9 9 9 9 9 9 9 9 9 9 9 9 9 9 9 9
9 9 9 9 9 9 9 9 9 9 9 9 9 9 9 9 9 9 9 9 9 9 9 9 9 9 9 9 9 9 9 9 9 9 9 9 9
9 9 9 9 9 9 9 9 9 9 9 9 9 9 9 9 9 9 9 9 9 9 9 9 9 9 9 9 9 9 9 9 9 9 9 9 9
9 9 9 9 9 9 9 9 9 9 9 9 9 9 9 9 9 9 9 9 9 9 9 9 9 9 9 9 9 9 9 9 9 9 9 9 9
9 9 9 9 9 9 9 9 9 9 9 9 9 9 9 9 9 9 9 9 9 9 9 9 9 9 9 9 9 9 9 9 9 9 9 9 9
9 9 9 9 9 9 9 9 9 9 9 9 9 9 9 9 9 9 9 9 9 9 9 9 9 9 9 9 9 9 9 9 9 9 9 9 9

dy	bug	fan	tas
tic	pen	man	ship
con	sis	tent	At
lan	tic	bas	ket
ball	con	gress	man
dis	in	fect	sev
en	ty		

<u>Word list:</u>

Dependent	de pen dent
Potency	po ten cy
Diminish	dim min ish
Apprehend	ap pre hend
Volcanic	vol can ic
Almanac	al man ac
Investment	in vest ment
Republic	re pub lic
Democrat	dem o crat
Ladybug	la dy bug
Fantastic	fan tas tic
Penmanship	pen man ship
Consistent	con sis tent
Atlantic	At lan tic
Basketball	bas ket ball
Congressman	con gress man
Disinfect	dis in fect
Seventy	sev en ty

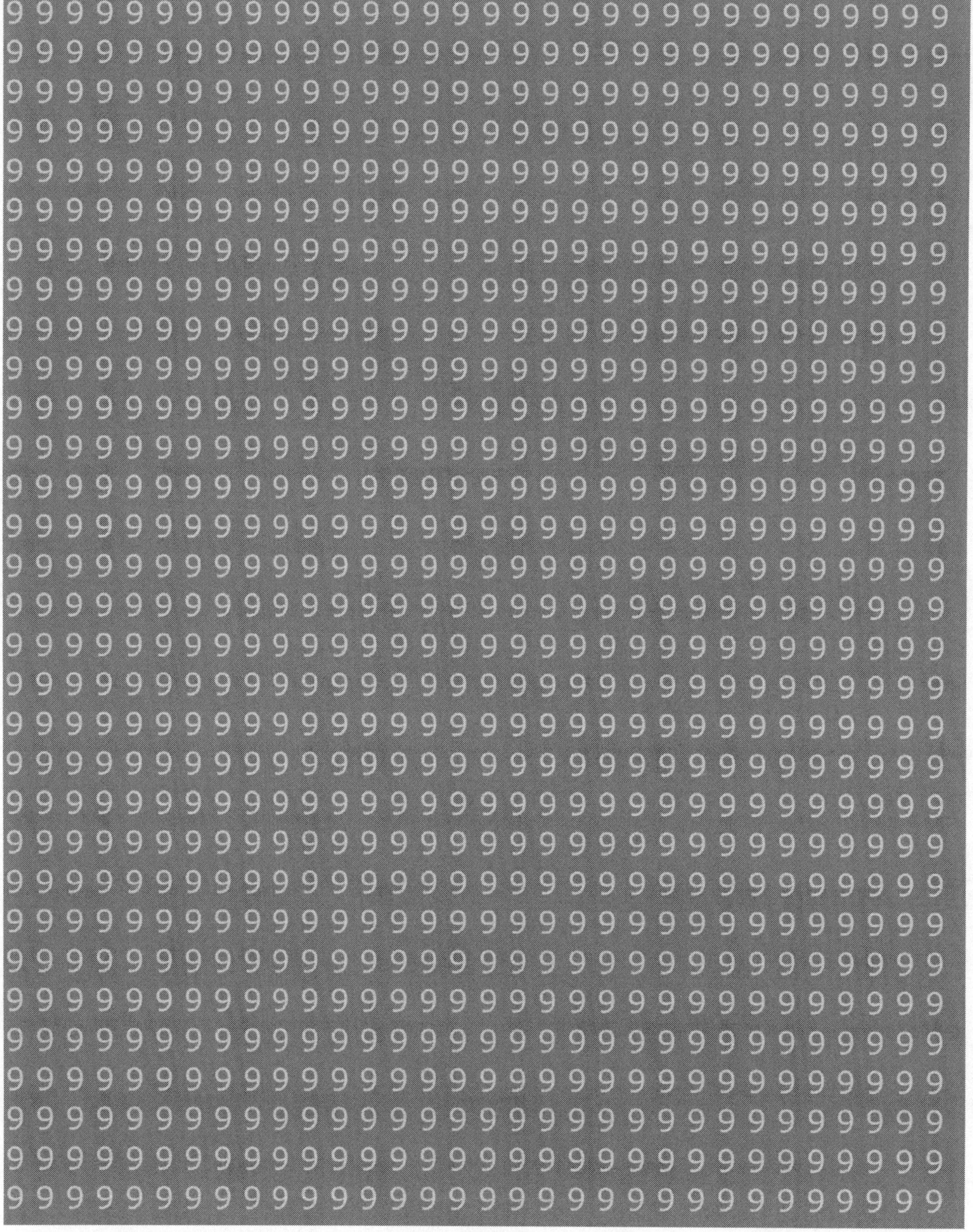

Board #1

dependent	de	pen	dent
potency			
diminish			

Board #2

apprehend			
volcanic			
almanac			

9 9 9 9 9 9 9 9 9 9 9 9 9 9 9 9 9 9 9 9 9 9 9 9 9 9 9 9 9 9 9 9
9 9 9 9 9 9 9 9 9 9 9 9 9 9 9 9 9 9 9 9 9 9 9 9 9 9 9 9 9 9 9 9
9 9 9 9 9 9 9 9 9 9 9 9 9 9 9 9 9 9 9 9 9 9 9 9 9 9 9 9 9 9 9 9
9 9 9 9 9 9 9 9 9 9 9 9 9 9 9 9 9 9 9 9 9 9 9 9 9 9 9 9 9 9 9 9
9 9 9 9 9 9 9 9 9 9 9 9 9 9 9 9 9 9 9 9 9 9 9 9 9 9 9 9 9 9 9 9
9 9 9 9 9 9 9 9 9 9 9 9 9 9 9 9 9 9 9 9 9 9 9 9 9 9 9 9 9 9 9 9
9 9 9 9 9 9 9 9 9 9 9 9 9 9 9 9 9 9 9 9 9 9 9 9 9 9 9 9 9 9 9 9
9 9 9 9 9 9 9 9 9 9 9 9 9 9 9 9 9 9 9 9 9 9 9 9 9 9 9 9 9 9 9 9
9 9 9 9 9 9 9 9 9 9 9 9 9 9 9 9 9 9 9 9 9 9 9 9 9 9 9 9 9 9 9 9
9 9 9 9 9 9 9 9 9 9 9 9 9 9 9 9 9 9 9 9 9 9 9 9 9 9 9 9 9 9 9 9
9 9 9 9 9 9 9 9 9 9 9 9 9 9 9 9 9 9 9 9 9 9 9 9 9 9 9 9 9 9 9 9
9 9 9 9 9 9 9 9 9 9 9 9 9 9 9 9 9 9 9 9 9 9 9 9 9 9 9 9 9 9 9 9
9 9 9 9 9 9 9 9 9 9 9 9 9 9 9 9 9 9 9 9 9 9 9 9 9 9 9 9 9 9 9 9
9 9 9 9 9 9 9 9 9 9 9 9 9 9 9 9 9 9 9 9 9 9 9 9 9 9 9 9 9 9 9 9
9 9 9 9 9 9 9 9 9 9 9 9 9 9 9 9 9 9 9 9 9 9 9 9 9 9 9 9 9 9 9 9
9 9 9 9 9 9 9 9 9 9 9 9 9 9 9 9 9 9 9 9 9 9 9 9 9 9 9 9 9 9 9 9
9 9 9 9 9 9 9 9 9 9 9 9 9 9 9 9 9 9 9 9 9 9 9 9 9 9 9 9 9 9 9 9
9 9 9 9 9 9 9 9 9 9 9 9 9 9 9 9 9 9 9 9 9 9 9 9 9 9 9 9 9 9 9 9
9 9 9 9 9 9 9 9 9 9 9 9 9 9 9 9 9 9 9 9 9 9 9 9 9 9 9 9 9 9 9 9
9 9 9 9 9 9 9 9 9 9 9 9 9 9 9 9 9 9 9 9 9 9 9 9 9 9 9 9 9 9 9 9
9 9 9 9 9 9 9 9 9 9 9 9 9 9 9 9 9 9 9 9 9 9 9 9 9 9 9 9 9 9 9 9
9 9 9 9 9 9 9 9 9 9 9 9 9 9 9 9 9 9 9 9 9 9 9 9 9 9 9 9 9 9 9 9
9 9 9 9 9 9 9 9 9 9 9 9 9 9 9 9 9 9 9 9 9 9 9 9 9 9 9 9 9 9 9 9
9 9 9 9 9 9 9 9 9 9 9 9 9 9 9 9 9 9 9 9 9 9 9 9 9 9 9 9 9 9 9 9
9 9 9 9 9 9 9 9 9 9 9 9 9 9 9 9 9 9 9 9 9 9 9 9 9 9 9 9 9 9 9 9
9 9 9 9 9 9 9 9 9 9 9 9 9 9 9 9 9 9 9 9 9 9 9 9 9 9 9 9 9 9 9 9
9 9 9 9 9 9 9 9 9 9 9 9 9 9 9 9 9 9 9 9 9 9 9 9 9 9 9 9 9 9 9 9
9 9 9 9 9 9 9 9 9 9 9 9 9 9 9 9 9 9 9 9 9 9 9 9 9 9 9 9 9 9 9 9
9 9 9 9 9 9 9 9 9 9 9 9 9 9 9 9 9 9 9 9 9 9 9 9 9 9 9 9 9 9 9 9

Board #1

consistent	con	sis	tent
Atlantic			
basketball			

Board #2

congressman			
disinfect			
seventy			

9 9 9 9 9 9 9 9 9 9 9 9 9 9 9 9 9 9 9 9 9 9 9 9 9 9 9 9 9 9 9 9 9 9 9 9
9 9 9 9 9 9 9 9 9 9 9 9 9 9 9 9 9 9 9 9 9 9 9 9 9 9 9 9 9 9 9 9 9 9 9 9
9 9 9 9 9 9 9 9 9 9 9 9 9 9 9 9 9 9 9 9 9 9 9 9 9 9 9 9 9 9 9 9 9 9 9 9
9 9 9 9 9 9 9 9 9 9 9 9 9 9 9 9 9 9 9 9 9 9 9 9 9 9 9 9 9 9 9 9 9 9 9 9
9 9 9 9 9 9 9 9 9 9 9 9 9 9 9 9 9 9 9 9 9 9 9 9 9 9 9 9 9 9 9 9 9 9 9 9
9 9 9 9 9 9 9 9 9 9 9 9 9 9 9 9 9 9 9 9 9 9 9 9 9 9 9 9 9 9 9 9 9 9 9 9
9 9 9 9 9 9 9 9 9 9 9 9 9 9 9 9 9 9 9 9 9 9 9 9 9 9 9 9 9 9 9 9 9 9 9 9
9 9 9 9 9 9 9 9 9 9 9 9 9 9 9 9 9 9 9 9 9 9 9 9 9 9 9 9 9 9 9 9 9 9 9 9
9 9 9 9 9 9 9 9 9 9 9 9 9 9 9 9 9 9 9 9 9 9 9 9 9 9 9 9 9 9 9 9 9 9 9 9
9 9 9 9 9 9 9 9 9 9 9 9 9 9 9 9 9 9 9 9 9 9 9 9 9 9 9 9 9 9 9 9 9 9 9 9
9 9 9 9 9 9 9 9 9 9 9 9 9 9 9 9 9 9 9 9 9 9 9 9 9 9 9 9 9 9 9 9 9 9 9 9
9 9 9 9 9 9 9 9 9 9 9 9 9 9 9 9 9 9 9 9 9 9 9 9 9 9 9 9 9 9 9 9 9 9 9 9
9 9 9 9 9 9 9 9 9 9 9 9 9 9 9 9 9 9 9 9 9 9 9 9 9 9 9 9 9 9 9 9 9 9 9 9
9 9 9 9 9 9 9 9 9 9 9 9 9 9 9 9 9 9 9 9 9 9 9 9 9 9 9 9 9 9 9 9 9 9 9 9
9 9 9 9 9 9 9 9 9 9 9 9 9 9 9 9 9 9 9 9 9 9 9 9 9 9 9 9 9 9 9 9 9 9 9 9
9 9 9 9 9 9 9 9 9 9 9 9 9 9 9 9 9 9 9 9 9 9 9 9 9 9 9 9 9 9 9 9 9 9 9 9
9 9 9 9 9 9 9 9 9 9 9 9 9 9 9 9 9 9 9 9 9 9 9 9 9 9 9 9 9 9 9 9 9 9 9 9
9 9 9 9 9 9 9 9 9 9 9 9 9 9 9 9 9 9 9 9 9 9 9 9 9 9 9 9 9 9 9 9 9 9 9 9
9 9 9 9 9 9 9 9 9 9 9 9 9 9 9 9 9 9 9 9 9 9 9 9 9 9 9 9 9 9 9 9 9 9 9 9
9 9 9 9 9 9 9 9 9 9 9 9 9 9 9 9 9 9 9 9 9 9 9 9 9 9 9 9 9 9 9 9 9 9 9 9
9 9 9 9 9 9 9 9 9 9 9 9 9 9 9 9 9 9 9 9 9 9 9 9 9 9 9 9 9 9 9 9 9 9 9 9
9 9 9 9 9 9 9 9 9 9 9 9 9 9 9 9 9 9 9 9 9 9 9 9 9 9 9 9 9 9 9 9 9 9 9 9
9 9 9 9 9 9 9 9 9 9 9 9 9 9 9 9 9 9 9 9 9 9 9 9 9 9 9 9 9 9 9 9 9 9 9 9
9 9 9 9 9 9 9 9 9 9 9 9 9 9 9 9 9 9 9 9 9 9 9 9 9 9 9 9 9 9 9 9 9 9 9 9
9 9 9 9 9 9 9 9 9 9 9 9 9 9 9 9 9 9 9 9 9 9 9 9 9 9 9 9 9 9 9 9 9 9 9 9
9 9 9 9 9 9 9 9 9 9 9 9 9 9 9 9 9 9 9 9 9 9 9 9 9 9 9 9 9 9 9 9 9 9 9 9
9 9 9 9 9 9 9 9 9 9 9 9 9 9 9 9 9 9 9 9 9 9 9 9 9 9 9 9 9 9 9 9 9 9 9 9
9 9 9 9 9 9 9 9 9 9 9 9 9 9 9 9 9 9 9 9 9 9 9 9 9 9 9 9 9 9 9 9 9 9 9 9
9 9 9 9 9 9 9 9 9 9 9 9 9 9 9 9 9 9 9 9 9 9 9 9 9 9 9 9 9 9 9 9 9 9 9 9
9 9 9 9 9 9 9 9 9 9 9 9 9 9 9 9 9 9 9 9 9 9 9 9 9 9 9 9 9 9 9 9 9 9 9 9

Board #1

investment	in	vest	ment
republic			
democrat			

Board #2

ladybug			
fantastic			
penmanship			

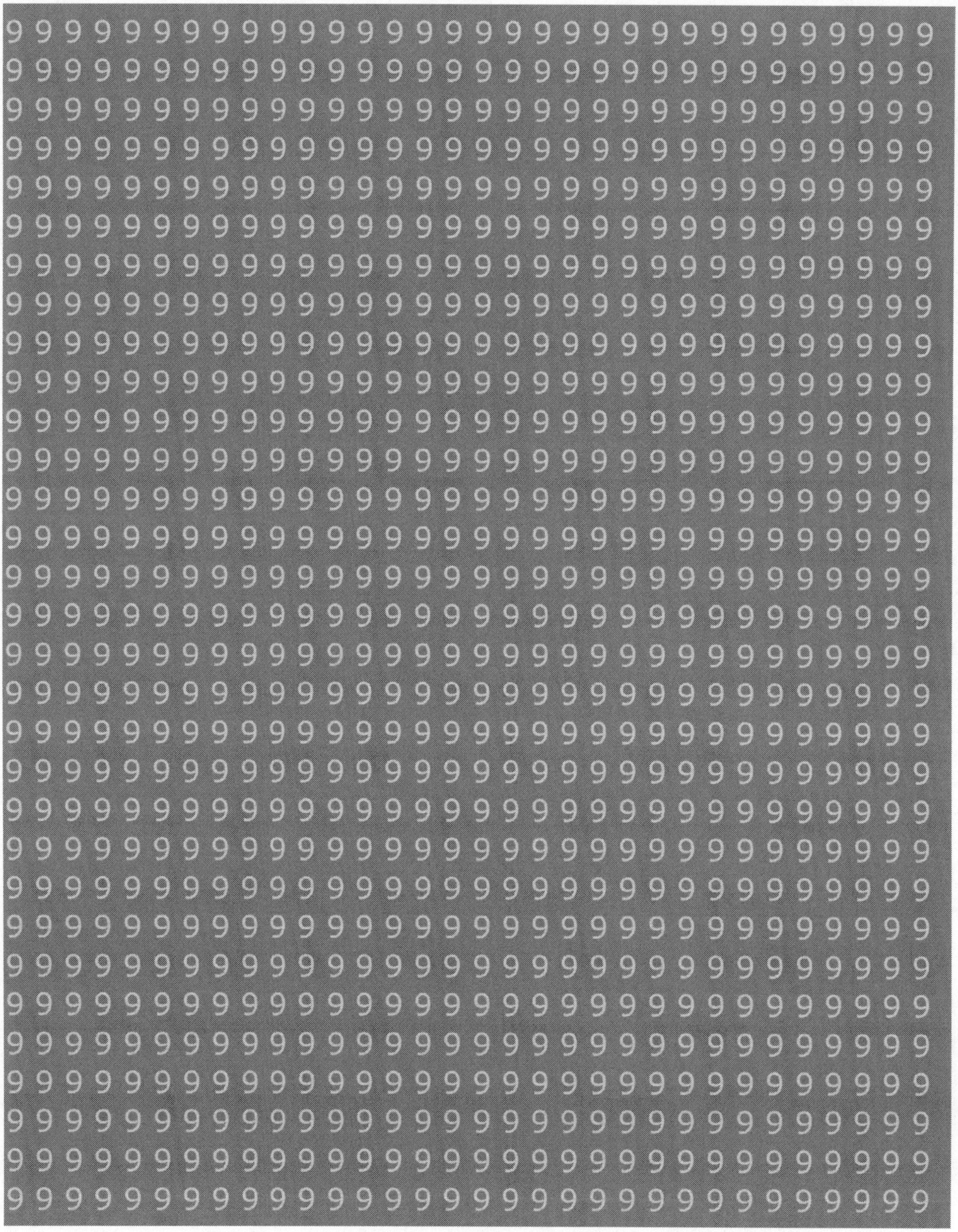

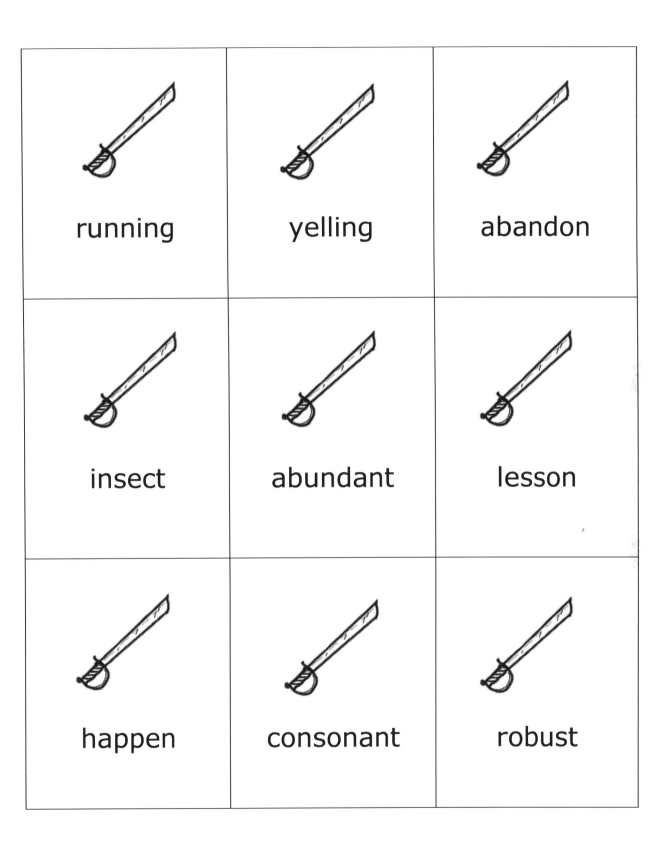

running

yelling

abandon

insect

abundant

lesson

happen

consonant

robust

10 10 10 10 10 10 10 10 10 10 10 10 10 10 10 10 10 10 10
10 10 10 10 10 10 10 10 10 10 10 10 10 10 10 10 10 10 10
10 10 10 10 10 10 10 10 10 10 10 10 10 10 10 10 10 10 10
10 10 10 10 10 10 10 10 10 10 10 10 10 10 10 10 10 10 10
10 10 10 10 10 10 10 10 10 10 10 10 10 10 10 10 10 10 10
10 10 10 10 10 10 10 10 10 10 10 10 10 10 10 10 10 10 10
10 10 10 10 10 10 10 10 10 10 10 10 10 10 10 10 10 10 10
10 10 10 10 10 10 10 10 10 10 10 10 10 10 10 10 10 10 10
10 10 10 10 10 10 10 10 10 10 10 10 10 10 10 10 10 10 10
10 10 10 10 10 10 10 10 10 10 10 10 10 10 10 10 10 10 10
10 10 10 10 10 10 10 10 10 10 10 10 10 10 10 10 10 10 10
10 10 10 10 10 10 10 10 10 10 10 10 10 10 10 10 10 10 10
10 10 10 10 10 10 10 10 10 10 10 10 10 10 10 10 10 10 10
10 10 10 10 10 10 10 10 10 10 10 10 10 10 10 10 10 10 10
10 10 10 10 10 10 10 10 10 10 10 10 10 10 10 10 10 10 10
10 10 10 10 10 10 10 10 10 10 10 10 10 10 10 10 10 10 10
10 10 10 10 10 10 10 10 10 10 10 10 10 10 10 10 10 10 10
10 10 10 10 10 10 10 10 10 10 10 10 10 10 10 10 10 10 10
10 10 10 10 10 10 10 10 10 10 10 10 10 10 10 10 10 10 10
10 10 10 10 10 10 10 10 10 10 10 10 10 10 10 10 10 10 10
10 10 10 10 10 10 10 10 10 10 10 10 10 10 10 10 10 10 10
10 10 10 10 10 10 10 10 10 10 10 10 10 10 10 10 10 10 10
10 10 10 10 10 10 10 10 10 10 10 10 10 10 10 10 10 10 10
10 10 10 10 10 10 10 10 10 10 10 10 10 10 10 10 10 10 10
10 10 10 10 10 10 10 10 10 10 10 10 10 10 10 10 10 10 10
10 10 10 10 10 10 10 10 10 10 10 10 10 10 10 10 10 10 10
10 10 10 10 10 10 10 10 10 10 10 10 10 10 10 10 10 10 10
10 10 10 10 10 10 10 10 10 10 10 10 10 10 10 10 10 10 10
10 10 10 10 10 10 10 10 10 10 10 10 10 10 10 10 10 10 10
10 10 10 10 10 10 10 10 10 10 10 10 10 10 10 10 10 10 10
10 10 10 10 10 10 10 10 10 10 10 10 10 10 10 10 10 10 10
10 10 10 10 10 10 10 10 10 10 10 10 10 10 10 10 10 10 10
10 10 10 10 10 10 10 10 10 10 10 10 10 10 10 10 10 10 10

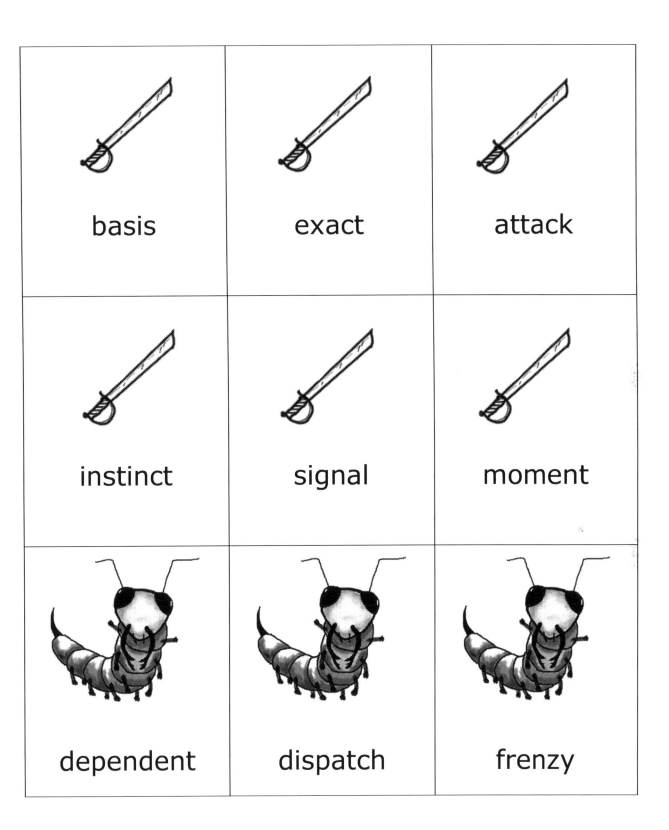

basis

exact

attack

instinct

signal

moment

dependent

dispatch

frenzy

10 10 10 10 10 10 10 10 10 10 10 10 10 10 10 10 10 10
10 10 10 10 10 10 10 10 10 10 10 10 10 10 10 10 10 10
10 10 10 10 10 10 10 10 10 10 10 10 10 10 10 10 10 10
10 10 10 10 10 10 10 10 10 10 10 10 10 10 10 10 10 10
10 10 10 10 10 10 10 10 10 10 10 10 10 10 10 10 10 10
10 10 10 10 10 10 10 10 10 10 10 10 10 10 10 10 10 10
10 10 10 10 10 10 10 10 10 10 10 10 10 10 10 10 10 10
10 10 10 10 10 10 10 10 10 10 10 10 10 10 10 10 10 10
10 10 10 10 10 10 10 10 10 10 10 10 10 10 10 10 10 10
10 10 10 10 10 10 10 10 10 10 10 10 10 10 10 10 10 10
10 10 10 10 10 10 10 10 10 10 10 10 10 10 10 10 10 10
10 10 10 10 10 10 10 10 10 10 10 10 10 10 10 10 10 10
10 10 10 10 10 10 10 10 10 10 10 10 10 10 10 10 10 10
10 10 10 10 10 10 10 10 10 10 10 10 10 10 10 10 10 10
10 10 10 10 10 10 10 10 10 10 10 10 10 10 10 10 10 10
10 10 10 10 10 10 10 10 10 10 10 10 10 10 10 10 10 10
10 10 10 10 10 10 10 10 10 10 10 10 10 10 10 10 10 10
10 10 10 10 10 10 10 10 10 10 10 10 10 10 10 10 10 10
10 10 10 10 10 10 10 10 10 10 10 10 10 10 10 10 10 10
10 10 10 10 10 10 10 10 10 10 10 10 10 10 10 10 10 10
10 10 10 10 10 10 10 10 10 10 10 10 10 10 10 10 10 10
10 10 10 10 10 10 10 10 10 10 10 10 10 10 10 10 10 10
10 10 10 10 10 10 10 10 10 10 10 10 10 10 10 10 10 10
10 10 10 10 10 10 10 10 10 10 10 10 10 10 10 10 10 10
10 10 10 10 10 10 10 10 10 10 10 10 10 10 10 10 10 10
10 10 10 10 10 10 10 10 10 10 10 10 10 10 10 10 10 10
10 10 10 10 10 10 10 10 10 10 10 10 10 10 10 10 10 10
10 10 10 10 10 10 10 10 10 10 10 10 10 10 10 10 10 10
10 10 10 10 10 10 10 10 10 10 10 10 10 10 10 10 10 10
10 10 10 10 10 10 10 10 10 10 10 10 10 10 10 10 10 10
10 10 10 10 10 10 10 10 10 10 10 10 10 10 10 10 10 10

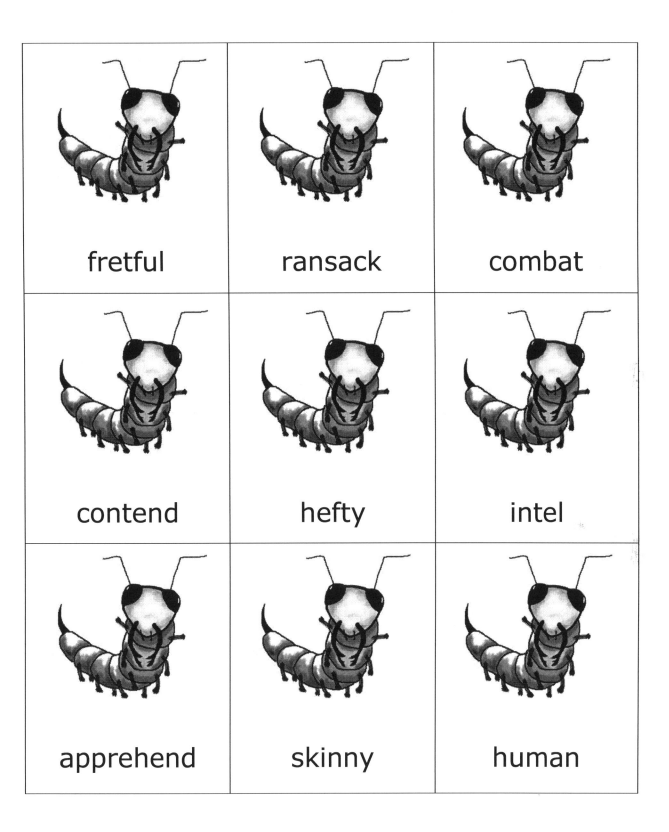

fretful	ransack	combat
contend	hefty	intel
apprehend	skinny	human

10 10 10 10 10 10 10 10 10 10 10 10 10 10 10 10 10 10
10 10 10 10 10 10 10 10 10 10 10 10 10 10 10 10 10 10
10 10 10 10 10 10 10 10 10 10 10 10 10 10 10 10 10 10
10 10 10 10 10 10 10 10 10 10 10 10 10 10 10 10 10 10
10 10 10 10 10 10 10 10 10 10 10 10 10 10 10 10 10 10
10 10 10 10 10 10 10 10 10 10 10 10 10 10 10 10 10 10
10 10 10 10 10 10 10 10 10 10 10 10 10 10 10 10 10 10
10 10 10 10 10 10 10 10 10 10 10 10 10 10 10 10 10 10
10 10 10 10 10 10 10 10 10 10 10 10 10 10 10 10 10 10
10 10 10 10 10 10 10 10 10 10 10 10 10 10 10 10 10 10
10 10 10 10 10 10 10 10 10 10 10 10 10 10 10 10 10 10
10 10 10 10 10 10 10 10 10 10 10 10 10 10 10 10 10 10
10 10 10 10 10 10 10 10 10 10 10 10 10 10 10 10 10 10
10 10 10 10 10 10 10 10 10 10 10 10 10 10 10 10 10 10
10 10 10 10 10 10 10 10 10 10 10 10 10 10 10 10 10 10
10 10 10 10 10 10 10 10 10 10 10 10 10 10 10 10 10 10
10 10 10 10 10 10 10 10 10 10 10 10 10 10 10 10 10 10
10 10 10 10 10 10 10 10 10 10 10 10 10 10 10 10 10 10
10 10 10 10 10 10 10 10 10 10 10 10 10 10 10 10 10 10
10 10 10 10 10 10 10 10 10 10 10 10 10 10 10 10 10 10
10 10 10 10 10 10 10 10 10 10 10 10 10 10 10 10 10 10
10 10 10 10 10 10 10 10 10 10 10 10 10 10 10 10 10 10
10 10 10 10 10 10 10 10 10 10 10 10 10 10 10 10 10 10
10 10 10 10 10 10 10 10 10 10 10 10 10 10 10 10 10 10
10 10 10 10 10 10 10 10 10 10 10 10 10 10 10 10 10 10
10 10 10 10 10 10 10 10 10 10 10 10 10 10 10 10 10 10
10 10 10 10 10 10 10 10 10 10 10 10 10 10 10 10 10 10
10 10 10 10 10 10 10 10 10 10 10 10 10 10 10 10 10 10
10 10 10 10 10 10 10 10 10 10 10 10 10 10 10 10 10 10
10 10 10 10 10 10 10 10 10 10 10 10 10 10 10 10 10 10
10 10 10 10 10 10 10 10 10 10 10 10 10 10 10 10 10 10
10 10 10 10 10 10 10 10 10 10 10 10 10 10 10 10 10 10
10 10 10 10 10 10 10 10 10 10 10 10 10 10 10 10 10 10

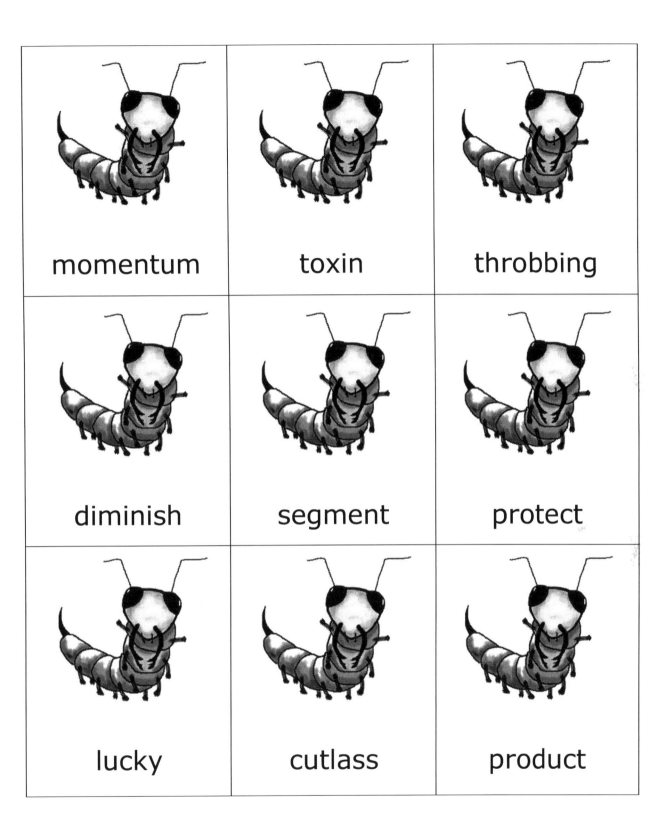

momentum	toxin	throbbing
diminish	segment	protect
lucky	cutlass	product

10 10 10 10 10 10 10 10 10 10 10 10 10 10 10 10 10 10
10 10 10 10 10 10 10 10 10 10 10 10 10 10 10 10 10 10
10 10 10 10 10 10 10 10 10 10 10 10 10 10 10 10 10 10
10 10 10 10 10 10 10 10 10 10 10 10 10 10 10 10 10 10
10 10 10 10 10 10 10 10 10 10 10 10 10 10 10 10 10 10
10 10 10 10 10 10 10 10 10 10 10 10 10 10 10 10 10 10
10 10 10 10 10 10 10 10 10 10 10 10 10 10 10 10 10 10
10 10 10 10 10 10 10 10 10 10 10 10 10 10 10 10 10 10
10 10 10 10 10 10 10 10 10 10 10 10 10 10 10 10 10 10
10 10 10 10 10 10 10 10 10 10 10 10 10 10 10 10 10 10
10 10 10 10 10 10 10 10 10 10 10 10 10 10 10 10 10 10
10 10 10 10 10 10 10 10 10 10 10 10 10 10 10 10 10 10
10 10 10 10 10 10 10 10 10 10 10 10 10 10 10 10 10 10
10 10 10 10 10 10 10 10 10 10 10 10 10 10 10 10 10 10
10 10 10 10 10 10 10 10 10 10 10 10 10 10 10 10 10 10
10 10 10 10 10 10 10 10 10 10 10 10 10 10 10 10 10 10
10 10 10 10 10 10 10 10 10 10 10 10 10 10 10 10 10 10
10 10 10 10 10 10 10 10 10 10 10 10 10 10 10 10 10 10
10 10 10 10 10 10 10 10 10 10 10 10 10 10 10 10 10 10
10 10 10 10 10 10 10 10 10 10 10 10 10 10 10 10 10 10
10 10 10 10 10 10 10 10 10 10 10 10 10 10 10 10 10 10
10 10 10 10 10 10 10 10 10 10 10 10 10 10 10 10 10 10
10 10 10 10 10 10 10 10 10 10 10 10 10 10 10 10 10 10
10 10 10 10 10 10 10 10 10 10 10 10 10 10 10 10 10 10
10 10 10 10 10 10 10 10 10 10 10 10 10 10 10 10 10 10
10 10 10 10 10 10 10 10 10 10 10 10 10 10 10 10 10 10
10 10 10 10 10 10 10 10 10 10 10 10 10 10 10 10 10 10
10 10 10 10 10 10 10 10 10 10 10 10 10 10 10 10 10 10
10 10 10 10 10 10 10 10 10 10 10 10 10 10 10 10 10 10
10 10 10 10 10 10 10 10 10 10 10 10 10 10 10 10 10 10
10 10 10 10 10 10 10 10 10 10 10 10 10 10 10 10 10 10
10 10 10 10 10 10 10 10 10 10 10 10 10 10 10 10 10 10
10 10 10 10 10 10 10 10 10 10 10 10 10 10 10 10 10 10

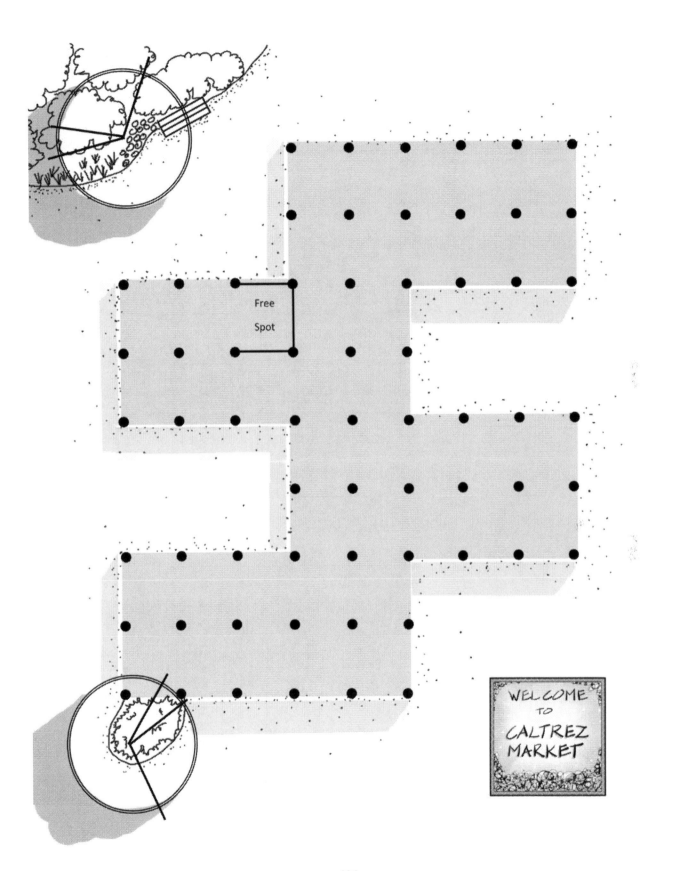

Free

Spot

WELCOME
TO
CALTREZ
MARKET

11 11 11 11 11 11 11 11 11 11 11 11 11 11 11 11
11 11 11 11 11 11 11 11 11 11 11 11 11 11 11 11
11 11 11 11 11 11 11 11 11 11 11 11 11 11 11 11
11 11 11 11 11 11 11 11 11 11 11 11 11 11 11 11
11 11 11 11 11 11 11 11 11 11 11 11 11 11 11 11
11 11 11 11 11 11 11 11 11 11 11 11 11 11 11 11
11 11 11 11 11 11 11 11 11 11 11 11 11 11 11 11
11 11 11 11 11 11 11 11 11 11 11 11 11 11 11 11
11 11 11 11 11 11 11 11 11 11 11 11 11 11 11 11
11 11 11 11 11 11 11 11 11 11 11 11 11 11 11 11
11 11 11 11 11 11 11 11 11 11 11 11 11 11 11 11
11 11 11 11 11 11 11 11 11 11 11 11 11 11 11 11
11 11 11 11 11 11 11 11 11 11 11 11 11 11 11 11
11 11 11 11 11 11 11 11 11 11 11 11 11 11 11 11
11 11 11 11 11 11 11 11 11 11 11 11 11 11 11 11
11 11 11 11 11 11 11 11 11 11 11 11 11 11 11 11
11 11 11 11 11 11 11 11 11 11 11 11 11 11 11 11
11 11 11 11 11 11 11 11 11 11 11 11 11 11 11 11
11 11 11 11 11 11 11 11 11 11 11 11 11 11 11 11
11 11 11 11 11 11 11 11 11 11 11 11 11 11 11 11
11 11 11 11 11 11 11 11 11 11 11 11 11 11 11 11
11 11 11 11 11 11 11 11 11 11 11 11 11 11 11 11
11 11 11 11 11 11 11 11 11 11 11 11 11 11 11 11
11 11 11 11 11 11 11 11 11 11 11 11 11 11 11 11
11 11 11 11 11 11 11 11 11 11 11 11 11 11 11 11
11 11 11 11 11 11 11 11 11 11 11 11 11 11 11 11
11 11 11 11 11 11 11 11 11 11 11 11 11 11 11 11
11 11 11 11 11 11 11 11 11 11 11 11 11 11 11 11
11 11 11 11 11 11 11 11 11 11 11 11 11 11 11 11
11 11 11 11 11 11 11 11 11 11 11 11 11 11 11 11
11 11 11 11 11 11 11 11 11 11 11 11 11 11 11 11

family	banana	Africa	consonant
animal	seventy	Jessica	potato
amazing	musical	Florida	tomato
vanilla	Mexico	hospital	innocent
accident	unity	octopus	medical
punishment	tropical	paradox	coconut

11 11 11 11 11 11 11 11 11 11 11 11 11 11 11 11
11 11 11 11 11 11 11 11 11 11 11 11 11 11 11 11
11 11 11 11 11 11 11 11 11 11 11 11 11 11 11 11
11 11 11 11 11 11 11 11 11 11 11 11 11 11 11 11
11 11 11 11 11 11 11 11 11 11 11 11 11 11 11 11
11 11 11 11 11 11 11 11 11 11 11 11 11 11 11 11
11 11 11 11 11 11 11 11 11 11 11 11 11 11 11 11
11 11 11 11 11 11 11 11 11 11 11 11 11 11 11 11
11 11 11 11 11 11 11 11 11 11 11 11 11 11 11 11
11 11 11 11 11 11 11 11 11 11 11 11 11 11 11 11
11 11 11 11 11 11 11 11 11 11 11 11 11 11 11 11
11 11 11 11 11 11 11 11 11 11 11 11 11 11 11 11
11 11 11 11 11 11 11 11 11 11 11 11 11 11 11 11
11 11 11 11 11 11 11 11 11 11 11 11 11 11 11 11
11 11 11 11 11 11 11 11 11 11 11 11 11 11 11 11
11 11 11 11 11 11 11 11 11 11 11 11 11 11 11 11
11 11 11 11 11 11 11 11 11 11 11 11 11 11 11 11
11 11 11 11 11 11 11 11 11 11 11 11 11 11 11 11
11 11 11 11 11 11 11 11 11 11 11 11 11 11 11 11
11 11 11 11 11 11 11 11 11 11 11 11 11 11 11 11
11 11 11 11 11 11 11 11 11 11 11 11 11 11 11 11
11 11 11 11 11 11 11 11 11 11 11 11 11 11 11 11
11 11 11 11 11 11 11 11 11 11 11 11 11 11 11 11
11 11 11 11 11 11 11 11 11 11 11 11 11 11 11 11
11 11 11 11 11 11 11 11 11 11 11 11 11 11 11 11
11 11 11 11 11 11 11 11 11 11 11 11 11 11 11 11
11 11 11 11 11 11 11 11 11 11 11 11 11 11 11 11
11 11 11 11 11 11 11 11 11 11 11 11 11 11 11 11
11 11 11 11 11 11 11 11 11 11 11 11 11 11 11 11
11 11 11 11 11 11 11 11 11 11 11 11 11 11 11 11
11 11 11 11 11 11 11 11 11 11 11 11 11 11 11 11
11 11 11 11 11 11 11 11 11 11 11 11 11 11 11 11
11 11 11 11 11 11 11 11 11 11 11 11 11 11 11 11

Alaska	skeleton	ebony	Mexican
biblical	trinity	mitosis	enemy
accomplish	instrument	compliment	cabinet
Omaha	balcony	silicon	decimal
vitamin	canopy	dilemma	abandon
elastic	sentiment	equipment	diploma

11 11 11 11 11 11 11 11 11 11 11 11 11 11 11 11
11 11 11 11 11 11 11 11 11 11 11 11 11 11 11 11
11 11 11 11 11 11 11 11 11 11 11 11 11 11 11 11
11 11 11 11 11 11 11 11 11 11 11 11 11 11 11 11
11 11 11 11 11 11 11 11 11 11 11 11 11 11 11 11
11 11 11 11 11 11 11 11 11 11 11 11 11 11 11 11
11 11 11 11 11 11 11 11 11 11 11 11 11 11 11 11
11 11 11 11 11 11 11 11 11 11 11 11 11 11 11 11
11 11 11 11 11 11 11 11 11 11 11 11 11 11 11 11
11 11 11 11 11 11 11 11 11 11 11 11 11 11 11 11
11 11 11 11 11 11 11 11 11 11 11 11 11 11 11 11
11 11 11 11 11 11 11 11 11 11 11 11 11 11 11 11
11 11 11 11 11 11 11 11 11 11 11 11 11 11 11 11
11 11 11 11 11 11 11 11 11 11 11 11 11 11 11 11
11 11 11 11 11 11 11 11 11 11 11 11 11 11 11 11
11 11 11 11 11 11 11 11 11 11 11 11 11 11 11 11
11 11 11 11 11 11 11 11 11 11 11 11 11 11 11 11
11 11 11 11 11 11 11 11 11 11 11 11 11 11 11 11
11 11 11 11 11 11 11 11 11 11 11 11 11 11 11 11
11 11 11 11 11 11 11 11 11 11 11 11 11 11 11 11
11 11 11 11 11 11 11 11 11 11 11 11 11 11 11 11
11 11 11 11 11 11 11 11 11 11 11 11 11 11 11 11
11 11 11 11 11 11 11 11 11 11 11 11 11 11 11 11
11 11 11 11 11 11 11 11 11 11 11 11 11 11 11 11
11 11 11 11 11 11 11 11 11 11 11 11 11 11 11 11
11 11 11 11 11 11 11 11 11 11 11 11 11 11 11 11
11 11 11 11 11 11 11 11 11 11 11 11 11 11 11 11
11 11 11 11 11 11 11 11 11 11 11 11 11 11 11 11
11 11 11 11 11 11 11 11 11 11 11 11 11 11 11 11
11 11 11 11 11 11 11 11 11 11 11 11 11 11 11 11

Alamo	iconic	envelop	industry
policy	calculus	admonish	felony
cavity	ethical	density	evident
excellent	habitat	hexagon	apricot
entity	exotic	spatula	remedy
electron	domestic	benefit	activist

11 11 11 11 11 11 11 11 11 11 11 11 11 11 11 11
11 11 11 11 11 11 11 11 11 11 11 11 11 11 11 11
11 11 11 11 11 11 11 11 11 11 11 11 11 11 11 11
11 11 11 11 11 11 11 11 11 11 11 11 11 11 11 11
11 11 11 11 11 11 11 11 11 11 11 11 11 11 11 11
11 11 11 11 11 11 11 11 11 11 11 11 11 11 11 11
11 11 11 11 11 11 11 11 11 11 11 11 11 11 11 11
11 11 11 11 11 11 11 11 11 11 11 11 11 11 11 11
11 11 11 11 11 11 11 11 11 11 11 11 11 11 11 11
11 11 11 11 11 11 11 11 11 11 11 11 11 11 11 11
11 11 11 11 11 11 11 11 11 11 11 11 11 11 11 11
11 11 11 11 11 11 11 11 11 11 11 11 11 11 11 11
11 11 11 11 11 11 11 11 11 11 11 11 11 11 11 11
11 11 11 11 11 11 11 11 11 11 11 11 11 11 11 11
11 11 11 11 11 11 11 11 11 11 11 11 11 11 11 11
11 11 11 11 11 11 11 11 11 11 11 11 11 11 11 11
11 11 11 11 11 11 11 11 11 11 11 11 11 11 11 11
11 11 11 11 11 11 11 11 11 11 11 11 11 11 11 11
11 11 11 11 11 11 11 11 11 11 11 11 11 11 11 11
11 11 11 11 11 11 11 11 11 11 11 11 11 11 11 11
11 11 11 11 11 11 11 11 11 11 11 11 11 11 11 11
11 11 11 11 11 11 11 11 11 11 11 11 11 11 11 11
11 11 11 11 11 11 11 11 11 11 11 11 11 11 11 11
11 11 11 11 11 11 11 11 11 11 11 11 11 11 11 11
11 11 11 11 11 11 11 11 11 11 11 11 11 11 11 11
11 11 11 11 11 11 11 11 11 11 11 11 11 11 11 11
11 11 11 11 11 11 11 11 11 11 11 11 11 11 11 11
11 11 11 11 11 11 11 11 11 11 11 11 11 11 11 11
11 11 11 11 11 11 11 11 11 11 11 11 11 11 11 11
11 11 11 11 11 11 11 11 11 11 11 11 11 11 11 11
11 11 11 11 11 11 11 11 11 11 11 11 11 11 11 11
11 11 11 11 11 11 11 11 11 11 11 11 11 11 11 11
11 11 11 11 11 11 11 11 11 11 11 11 11 11 11 11

bay	lay	ray
hay	may	say
day	jay	way
pay	yay	away

12 12 12 12 12 12 12 12 12 12 12 12 12 12 12 12
12 12 12 12 12 12 12 12 12 12 12 12 12 12 12 12
12 12 12 12 12 12 12 12 12 12 12 12 12 12 12 12
12 12 12 12 12 12 12 12 12 12 12 12 12 12 12 12
12 12 12 12 12 12 12 12 12 12 12 12 12 12 12 12
12 12 12 12 12 12 12 12 12 12 12 12 12 12 12 12
12 12 12 12 12 12 12 12 12 12 12 12 12 12 12 12
12 12 12 12 12 12 12 12 12 12 12 12 12 12 12 12
12 12 12 12 12 12 12 12 12 12 12 12 12 12 12 12
12 12 12 12 12 12 12 12 12 12 12 12 12 12 12 12
12 12 12 12 12 12 12 12 12 12 12 12 12 12 12 12
12 12 12 12 12 12 12 12 12 12 12 12 12 12 12 12
12 12 12 12 12 12 12 12 12 12 12 12 12 12 12 12
12 12 12 12 12 12 12 12 12 12 12 12 12 12 12 12
12 12 12 12 12 12 12 12 12 12 12 12 12 12 12 12
12 12 12 12 12 12 12 12 12 12 12 12 12 12 12 12
12 12 12 12 12 12 12 12 12 12 12 12 12 12 12 12
12 12 12 12 12 12 12 12 12 12 12 12 12 12 12 12
12 12 12 12 12 12 12 12 12 12 12 12 12 12 12 12
12 12 12 12 12 12 12 12 12 12 12 12 12 12 12 12
12 12 12 12 12 12 12 12 12 12 12 12 12 12 12 12
12 12 12 12 12 12 12 12 12 12 12 12 12 12 12 12
12 12 12 12 12 12 12 12 12 12 12 12 12 12 12 12
12 12 12 12 12 12 12 12 12 12 12 12 12 12 12 12
12 12 12 12 12 12 12 12 12 12 12 12 12 12 12 12
12 12 12 12 12 12 12 12 12 12 12 12 12 12 12 12
12 12 12 12 12 12 12 12 12 12 12 12 12 12 12 12
12 12 12 12 12 12 12 12 12 12 12 12 12 12 12 12
12 12 12 12 12 12 12 12 12 12 12 12 12 12 12 12
12 12 12 12 12 12 12 12 12 12 12 12 12 12 12 12
12 12 12 12 12 12 12 12 12 12 12 12 12 12 12 12
12 12 12 12 12 12 12 12 12 12 12 12 12 12 12 12

stay	okay	sway
fray	play	tray
clay	pray	gray
inlay	decay	essay

12 12 12 12 12 12 12 12 12 12 12 12 12 12 12 12
12 12 12 12 12 12 12 12 12 12 12 12 12 12 12 12
12 12 12 12 12 12 12 12 12 12 12 12 12 12 12 12
12 12 12 12 12 12 12 12 12 12 12 12 12 12 12 12
12 12 12 12 12 12 12 12 12 12 12 12 12 12 12 12
12 12 12 12 12 12 12 12 12 12 12 12 12 12 12 12
12 12 12 12 12 12 12 12 12 12 12 12 12 12 12 12
12 12 12 12 12 12 12 12 12 12 12 12 12 12 12 12
12 12 12 12 12 12 12 12 12 12 12 12 12 12 12 12
12 12 12 12 12 12 12 12 12 12 12 12 12 12 12 12
12 12 12 12 12 12 12 12 12 12 12 12 12 12 12 12
12 12 12 12 12 12 12 12 12 12 12 12 12 12 12 12
12 12 12 12 12 12 12 12 12 12 12 12 12 12 12 12
12 12 12 12 12 12 12 12 12 12 12 12 12 12 12 12
12 12 12 12 12 12 12 12 12 12 12 12 12 12 12 12
12 12 12 12 12 12 12 12 12 12 12 12 12 12 12 12
12 12 12 12 12 12 12 12 12 12 12 12 12 12 12 12
12 12 12 12 12 12 12 12 12 12 12 12 12 12 12 12
12 12 12 12 12 12 12 12 12 12 12 12 12 12 12 12
12 12 12 12 12 12 12 12 12 12 12 12 12 12 12 12
12 12 12 12 12 12 12 12 12 12 12 12 12 12 12 12
12 12 12 12 12 12 12 12 12 12 12 12 12 12 12 12
12 12 12 12 12 12 12 12 12 12 12 12 12 12 12 12
12 12 12 12 12 12 12 12 12 12 12 12 12 12 12 12
12 12 12 12 12 12 12 12 12 12 12 12 12 12 12 12
12 12 12 12 12 12 12 12 12 12 12 12 12 12 12 12
12 12 12 12 12 12 12 12 12 12 12 12 12 12 12 12
12 12 12 12 12 12 12 12 12 12 12 12 12 12 12 12
12 12 12 12 12 12 12 12 12 12 12 12 12 12 12 12
12 12 12 12 12 12 12 12 12 12 12 12 12 12 12 12
12 12 12 12 12 12 12 12 12 12 12 12 12 12 12 12
12 12 12 12 12 12 12 12 12 12 12 12 12 12 12 12
12 12 12 12 12 12 12 12 12 12 12 12 12 12 12 12

delay	stray	today
spray	dismay	payday
anyway	bee	pee
see	fee	flee

12 12 12 12 12 12 12 12 12 12 12 12 12 12 12 12
12 12 12 12 12 12 12 12 12 12 12 12 12 12 12 12
12 12 12 12 12 12 12 12 12 12 12 12 12 12 12 12
12 12 12 12 12 12 12 12 12 12 12 12 12 12 12 12
12 12 12 12 12 12 12 12 12 12 12 12 12 12 12 12
12 12 12 12 12 12 12 12 12 12 12 12 12 12 12 12
12 12 12 12 12 12 12 12 12 12 12 12 12 12 12 12
12 12 12 12 12 12 12 12 12 12 12 12 12 12 12 12
12 12 12 12 12 12 12 12 12 12 12 12 12 12 12 12
12 12 12 12 12 12 12 12 12 12 12 12 12 12 12 12
12 12 12 12 12 12 12 12 12 12 12 12 12 12 12 12
12 12 12 12 12 12 12 12 12 12 12 12 12 12 12 12
12 12 12 12 12 12 12 12 12 12 12 12 12 12 12 12
12 12 12 12 12 12 12 12 12 12 12 12 12 12 12 12
12 12 12 12 12 12 12 12 12 12 12 12 12 12 12 12
12 12 12 12 12 12 12 12 12 12 12 12 12 12 12 12
12 12 12 12 12 12 12 12 12 12 12 12 12 12 12 12
12 12 12 12 12 12 12 12 12 12 12 12 12 12 12 12
12 12 12 12 12 12 12 12 12 12 12 12 12 12 12 12
12 12 12 12 12 12 12 12 12 12 12 12 12 12 12 12
12 12 12 12 12 12 12 12 12 12 12 12 12 12 12 12
12 12 12 12 12 12 12 12 12 12 12 12 12 12 12 12
12 12 12 12 12 12 12 12 12 12 12 12 12 12 12 12
12 12 12 12 12 12 12 12 12 12 12 12 12 12 12 12
12 12 12 12 12 12 12 12 12 12 12 12 12 12 12 12
12 12 12 12 12 12 12 12 12 12 12 12 12 12 12 12
12 12 12 12 12 12 12 12 12 12 12 12 12 12 12 12
12 12 12 12 12 12 12 12 12 12 12 12 12 12 12 12
12 12 12 12 12 12 12 12 12 12 12 12 12 12 12 12
12 12 12 12 12 12 12 12 12 12 12 12 12 12 12 12
12 12 12 12 12 12 12 12 12 12 12 12 12 12 12 12
12 12 12 12 12 12 12 12 12 12 12 12 12 12 12 12
12 12 12 12 12 12 12 12 12 12 12 12 12 12 12 12

thee	tree	flee
agree	spree	coffee
humvee	toffee	frisbee
fly	sky	cry

12 12 12 12 12 12 12 12 12 12 12 12 12 12 12 12
12 12 12 12 12 12 12 12 12 12 12 12 12 12 12 12
12 12 12 12 12 12 12 12 12 12 12 12 12 12 12 12
12 12 12 12 12 12 12 12 12 12 12 12 12 12 12 12
12 12 12 12 12 12 12 12 12 12 12 12 12 12 12 12
12 12 12 12 12 12 12 12 12 12 12 12 12 12 12 12
12 12 12 12 12 12 12 12 12 12 12 12 12 12 12 12
12 12 12 12 12 12 12 12 12 12 12 12 12 12 12 12
12 12 12 12 12 12 12 12 12 12 12 12 12 12 12 12
12 12 12 12 12 12 12 12 12 12 12 12 12 12 12 12
12 12 12 12 12 12 12 12 12 12 12 12 12 12 12 12
12 12 12 12 12 12 12 12 12 12 12 12 12 12 12 12
12 12 12 12 12 12 12 12 12 12 12 12 12 12 12 12
12 12 12 12 12 12 12 12 12 12 12 12 12 12 12 12
12 12 12 12 12 12 12 12 12 12 12 12 12 12 12 12
12 12 12 12 12 12 12 12 12 12 12 12 12 12 12 12
12 12 12 12 12 12 12 12 12 12 12 12 12 12 12 12
12 12 12 12 12 12 12 12 12 12 12 12 12 12 12 12
12 12 12 12 12 12 12 12 12 12 12 12 12 12 12 12
12 12 12 12 12 12 12 12 12 12 12 12 12 12 12 12
12 12 12 12 12 12 12 12 12 12 12 12 12 12 12 12
12 12 12 12 12 12 12 12 12 12 12 12 12 12 12 12
12 12 12 12 12 12 12 12 12 12 12 12 12 12 12 12
12 12 12 12 12 12 12 12 12 12 12 12 12 12 12 12
12 12 12 12 12 12 12 12 12 12 12 12 12 12 12 12
12 12 12 12 12 12 12 12 12 12 12 12 12 12 12 12
12 12 12 12 12 12 12 12 12 12 12 12 12 12 12 12
12 12 12 12 12 12 12 12 12 12 12 12 12 12 12 12
12 12 12 12 12 12 12 12 12 12 12 12 12 12 12 12
12 12 12 12 12 12 12 12 12 12 12 12 12 12 12 12
12 12 12 12 12 12 12 12 12 12 12 12 12 12 12 12
12 12 12 12 12 12 12 12 12 12 12 12 12 12 12 12

deny	rely	qualify
electrify	defy	liquify
amplify	unify	satisfy
petrify	apply	solidify

12 12 12 12 12 12 12 12 12 12 12 12 12 12 12 12
12 12 12 12 12 12 12 12 12 12 12 12 12 12 12 12
12 12 12 12 12 12 12 12 12 12 12 12 12 12 12 12
12 12 12 12 12 12 12 12 12 12 12 12 12 12 12 12
12 12 12 12 12 12 12 12 12 12 12 12 12 12 12 12
12 12 12 12 12 12 12 12 12 12 12 12 12 12 12 12
12 12 12 12 12 12 12 12 12 12 12 12 12 12 12 12
12 12 12 12 12 12 12 12 12 12 12 12 12 12 12 12
12 12 12 12 12 12 12 12 12 12 12 12 12 12 12 12
12 12 12 12 12 12 12 12 12 12 12 12 12 12 12 12
12 12 12 12 12 12 12 12 12 12 12 12 12 12 12 12
12 12 12 12 12 12 12 12 12 12 12 12 12 12 12 12
12 12 12 12 12 12 12 12 12 12 12 12 12 12 12 12
12 12 12 12 12 12 12 12 12 12 12 12 12 12 12 12
12 12 12 12 12 12 12 12 12 12 12 12 12 12 12 12
12 12 12 12 12 12 12 12 12 12 12 12 12 12 12 12
12 12 12 12 12 12 12 12 12 12 12 12 12 12 12 12
12 12 12 12 12 12 12 12 12 12 12 12 12 12 12 12
12 12 12 12 12 12 12 12 12 12 12 12 12 12 12 12
12 12 12 12 12 12 12 12 12 12 12 12 12 12 12 12
12 12 12 12 12 12 12 12 12 12 12 12 12 12 12 12
12 12 12 12 12 12 12 12 12 12 12 12 12 12 12 12
12 12 12 12 12 12 12 12 12 12 12 12 12 12 12 12
12 12 12 12 12 12 12 12 12 12 12 12 12 12 12 12
12 12 12 12 12 12 12 12 12 12 12 12 12 12 12 12
12 12 12 12 12 12 12 12 12 12 12 12 12 12 12 12
12 12 12 12 12 12 12 12 12 12 12 12 12 12 12 12
12 12 12 12 12 12 12 12 12 12 12 12 12 12 12 12
12 12 12 12 12 12 12 12 12 12 12 12 12 12 12 12
12 12 12 12 12 12 12 12 12 12 12 12 12 12 12 12
12 12 12 12 12 12 12 12 12 12 12 12 12 12 12 12
12 12 12 12 12 12 12 12 12 12 12 12 12 12 12 12

multiply	reply	dignify
signify	classify	testify

12 12 12 12 12 12 12 12 12 12 12 12 12 12 12 12
12 12 12 12 12 12 12 12 12 12 12 12 12 12 12 12
12 12 12 12 12 12 12 12 12 12 12 12 12 12 12 12
12 12 12 12 12 12 12 12 12 12 12 12 12 12 12 12
12 12 12 12 12 12 12 12 12 12 12 12 12 12 12 12
12 12 12 12 12 12 12 12 12 12 12 12 12 12 12 12
12 12 12 12 12 12 12 12 12 12 12 12 12 12 12 12
12 12 12 12 12 12 12 12 12 12 12 12 12 12 12 12
12 12 12 12 12 12 12 12 12 12 12 12 12 12 12 12
12 12 12 12 12 12 12 12 12 12 12 12 12 12 12 12
12 12 12 12 12 12 12 12 12 12 12 12 12 12 12 12
12 12 12 12 12 12 12 12 12 12 12 12 12 12 12 12
12 12 12 12 12 12 12 12 12 12 12 12 12 12 12 12
12 12 12 12 12 12 12 12 12 12 12 12 12 12 12 12
12 12 12 12 12 12 12 12 12 12 12 12 12 12 12 12
12 12 12 12 12 12 12 12 12 12 12 12 12 12 12 12
12 12 12 12 12 12 12 12 12 12 12 12 12 12 12 12
12 12 12 12 12 12 12 12 12 12 12 12 12 12 12 12
12 12 12 12 12 12 12 12 12 12 12 12 12 12 12 12
12 12 12 12 12 12 12 12 12 12 12 12 12 12 12 12
12 12 12 12 12 12 12 12 12 12 12 12 12 12 12 12
12 12 12 12 12 12 12 12 12 12 12 12 12 12 12 12
12 12 12 12 12 12 12 12 12 12 12 12 12 12 12 12
12 12 12 12 12 12 12 12 12 12 12 12 12 12 12 12
12 12 12 12 12 12 12 12 12 12 12 12 12 12 12 12
12 12 12 12 12 12 12 12 12 12 12 12 12 12 12 12
12 12 12 12 12 12 12 12 12 12 12 12 12 12 12 12
12 12 12 12 12 12 12 12 12 12 12 12 12 12 12 12
12 12 12 12 12 12 12 12 12 12 12 12 12 12 12 12
12 12 12 12 12 12 12 12 12 12 12 12 12 12 12 12

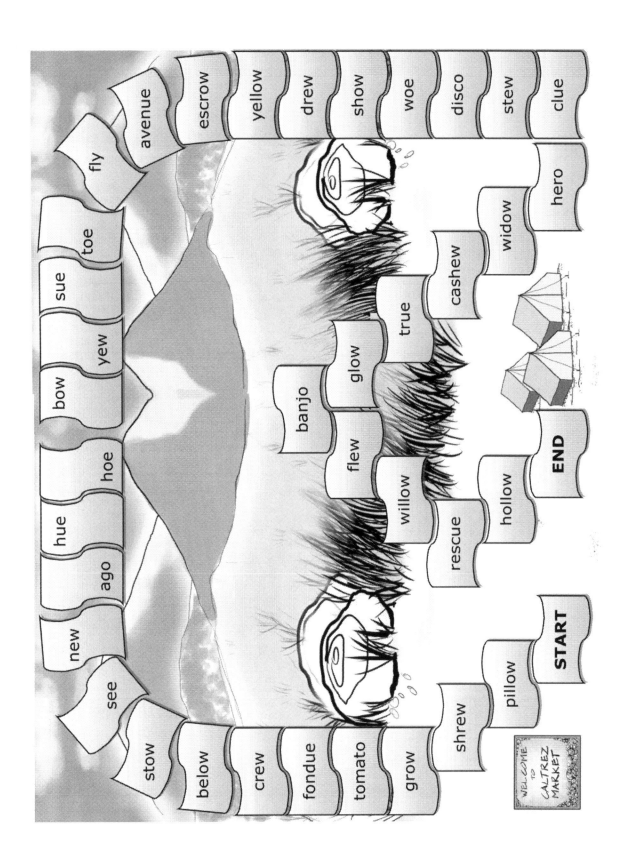

211

13 13 13 13 13 13 13 13 13 13 13 13 13 13 13 13
13 13 13 13 13 13 13 13 13 13 13 13 13 13 13 13
13 13 13 13 13 13 13 13 13 13 13 13 13 13 13 13
13 13 13 13 13 13 13 13 13 13 13 13 13 13 13 13
13 13 13 13 13 13 13 13 13 13 13 13 13 13 13 13
13 13 13 13 13 13 13 13 13 13 13 13 13 13 13 13
13 13 13 13 13 13 13 13 13 13 13 13 13 13 13 13
13 13 13 13 13 13 13 13 13 13 13 13 13 13 13 13
13 13 13 13 13 13 13 13 13 13 13 13 13 13 13 13
13 13 13 13 13 13 13 13 13 13 13 13 13 13 13 13
13 13 13 13 13 13 13 13 13 13 13 13 13 13 13 13
13 13 13 13 13 13 13 13 13 13 13 13 13 13 13 13
13 13 13 13 13 13 13 13 13 13 13 13 13 13 13 13
13 13 13 13 13 13 13 13 13 13 13 13 13 13 13 13
13 13 13 13 13 13 13 13 13 13 13 13 13 13 13 13
13 13 13 13 13 13 13 13 13 13 13 13 13 13 13 13
13 13 13 13 13 13 13 13 13 13 13 13 13 13 13 13
13 13 13 13 13 13 13 13 13 13 13 13 13 13 13 13
13 13 13 13 13 13 13 13 13 13 13 13 13 13 13 13
13 13 13 13 13 13 13 13 13 13 13 13 13 13 13 13
13 13 13 13 13 13 13 13 13 13 13 13 13 13 13 13
13 13 13 13 13 13 13 13 13 13 13 13 13 13 13 13
13 13 13 13 13 13 13 13 13 13 13 13 13 13 13 13
13 13 13 13 13 13 13 13 13 13 13 13 13 13 13 13
13 13 13 13 13 13 13 13 13 13 13 13 13 13 13 13
13 13 13 13 13 13 13 13 13 13 13 13 13 13 13 13
13 13 13 13 13 13 13 13 13 13 13 13 13 13 13 13
13 13 13 13 13 13 13 13 13 13 13 13 13 13 13 13
13 13 13 13 13 13 13 13 13 13 13 13 13 13 13 13
13 13 13 13 13 13 13 13 13 13 13 13 13 13 13 13

The land shifts. A jolt is felt. Go back one space.	The land shifts. A jolt is felt. Go back one space.	The land shifts. A jolt is felt. Go back one space.	The land shifts. A jolt is felt. Go back one space.
Stay with the ill dragon. Loose a turn.	Stay with the ill dragon. Loose a turn.	dew	few
pew	cue	due	sow
low	doe	foe	bee

13 13 13 13 13 13 13 13 13 13 13 13 13 13 13
13 13 13 13 13 13 13 13 13 13 13 13 13 13 13
13 13 13 13 13 13 13 13 13 13 13 13 13 13 13
13 13 13 13 13 13 13 13 13 13 13 13 13 13 13
13 13 13 13 13 13 13 13 13 13 13 13 13 13 13
13 13 13 13 13 13 13 13 13 13 13 13 13 13 13
13 13 13 13 13 13 13 13 13 13 13 13 13 13 13
13 13 13 13 13 13 13 13 13 13 13 13 13 13 13
13 13 13 13 13 13 13 13 13 13 13 13 13 13 13
13 13 13 13 13 13 13 13 13 13 13 13 13 13 13
13 13 13 13 13 13 13 13 13 13 13 13 13 13 13
13 13 13 13 13 13 13 13 13 13 13 13 13 13 13
13 13 13 13 13 13 13 13 13 13 13 13 13 13 13
13 13 13 13 13 13 13 13 13 13 13 13 13 13 13
13 13 13 13 13 13 13 13 13 13 13 13 13 13 13
13 13 13 13 13 13 13 13 13 13 13 13 13 13 13
13 13 13 13 13 13 13 13 13 13 13 13 13 13 13
13 13 13 13 13 13 13 13 13 13 13 13 13 13 13
13 13 13 13 13 13 13 13 13 13 13 13 13 13 13
13 13 13 13 13 13 13 13 13 13 13 13 13 13 13
13 13 13 13 13 13 13 13 13 13 13 13 13 13 13
13 13 13 13 13 13 13 13 13 13 13 13 13 13 13
13 13 13 13 13 13 13 13 13 13 13 13 13 13 13
13 13 13 13 13 13 13 13 13 13 13 13 13 13 13
13 13 13 13 13 13 13 13 13 13 13 13 13 13 13
13 13 13 13 13 13 13 13 13 13 13 13 13 13 13
13 13 13 13 13 13 13 13 13 13 13 13 13 13 13
13 13 13 13 13 13 13 13 13 13 13 13 13 13 13
13 13 13 13 13 13 13 13 13 13 13 13 13 13 13
13 13 13 13 13 13 13 13 13 13 13 13 13 13 13
13 13 13 13 13 13 13 13 13 13 13 13 13 13 13

flee	baby	maybe	try
comply	blew	brew	chew
grew	screw	mildew	residue
revenue	fescue	blue	blow

13 13 13 13 13 13 13 13 13 13 13 13 13 13 13 13
13 13 13 13 13 13 13 13 13 13 13 13 13 13 13 13
13 13 13 13 13 13 13 13 13 13 13 13 13 13 13 13
13 13 13 13 13 13 13 13 13 13 13 13 13 13 13 13
13 13 13 13 13 13 13 13 13 13 13 13 13 13 13 13
13 13 13 13 13 13 13 13 13 13 13 13 13 13 13 13
13 13 13 13 13 13 13 13 13 13 13 13 13 13 13 13
13 13 13 13 13 13 13 13 13 13 13 13 13 13 13 13
13 13 13 13 13 13 13 13 13 13 13 13 13 13 13 13
13 13 13 13 13 13 13 13 13 13 13 13 13 13 13 13
13 13 13 13 13 13 13 13 13 13 13 13 13 13 13 13
13 13 13 13 13 13 13 13 13 13 13 13 13 13 13 13
13 13 13 13 13 13 13 13 13 13 13 13 13 13 13 13
13 13 13 13 13 13 13 13 13 13 13 13 13 13 13 13
13 13 13 13 13 13 13 13 13 13 13 13 13 13 13 13
13 13 13 13 13 13 13 13 13 13 13 13 13 13 13 13
13 13 13 13 13 13 13 13 13 13 13 13 13 13 13 13
13 13 13 13 13 13 13 13 13 13 13 13 13 13 13 13
13 13 13 13 13 13 13 13 13 13 13 13 13 13 13 13
13 13 13 13 13 13 13 13 13 13 13 13 13 13 13 13
13 13 13 13 13 13 13 13 13 13 13 13 13 13 13 13
13 13 13 13 13 13 13 13 13 13 13 13 13 13 13 13
13 13 13 13 13 13 13 13 13 13 13 13 13 13 13 13
13 13 13 13 13 13 13 13 13 13 13 13 13 13 13 13
13 13 13 13 13 13 13 13 13 13 13 13 13 13 13 13
13 13 13 13 13 13 13 13 13 13 13 13 13 13 13 13
13 13 13 13 13 13 13 13 13 13 13 13 13 13 13 13
13 13 13 13 13 13 13 13 13 13 13 13 13 13 13 13
13 13 13 13 13 13 13 13 13 13 13 13 13 13 13 13
13 13 13 13 13 13 13 13 13 13 13 13 13 13 13 13
13 13 13 13 13 13 13 13 13 13 13 13 13 13 13 13
13 13 13 13 13 13 13 13 13 13 13 13 13 13 13 13

crow	flow	slow	snow
elbow	throw	mellow	minnow
window	calico	potato	fellow
follow	billow	glue	value

13 13 13 13 13 13 13 13 13 13 13 13 13 13 13 13
13 13 13 13 13 13 13 13 13 13 13 13 13 13 13 13
13 13 13 13 13 13 13 13 13 13 13 13 13 13 13 13
13 13 13 13 13 13 13 13 13 13 13 13 13 13 13 13
13 13 13 13 13 13 13 13 13 13 13 13 13 13 13 13
13 13 13 13 13 13 13 13 13 13 13 13 13 13 13 13
13 13 13 13 13 13 13 13 13 13 13 13 13 13 13 13
13 13 13 13 13 13 13 13 13 13 13 13 13 13 13 13
13 13 13 13 13 13 13 13 13 13 13 13 13 13 13 13
13 13 13 13 13 13 13 13 13 13 13 13 13 13 13 13
13 13 13 13 13 13 13 13 13 13 13 13 13 13 13 13
13 13 13 13 13 13 13 13 13 13 13 13 13 13 13 13
13 13 13 13 13 13 13 13 13 13 13 13 13 13 13 13
13 13 13 13 13 13 13 13 13 13 13 13 13 13 13 13
13 13 13 13 13 13 13 13 13 13 13 13 13 13 13 13
13 13 13 13 13 13 13 13 13 13 13 13 13 13 13 13
13 13 13 13 13 13 13 13 13 13 13 13 13 13 13 13
13 13 13 13 13 13 13 13 13 13 13 13 13 13 13 13
13 13 13 13 13 13 13 13 13 13 13 13 13 13 13 13
13 13 13 13 13 13 13 13 13 13 13 13 13 13 13 13
13 13 13 13 13 13 13 13 13 13 13 13 13 13 13 13
13 13 13 13 13 13 13 13 13 13 13 13 13 13 13 13
13 13 13 13 13 13 13 13 13 13 13 13 13 13 13 13
13 13 13 13 13 13 13 13 13 13 13 13 13 13 13 13
13 13 13 13 13 13 13 13 13 13 13 13 13 13 13 13
13 13 13 13 13 13 13 13 13 13 13 13 13 13 13 13
13 13 13 13 13 13 13 13 13 13 13 13 13 13 13 13
13 13 13 13 13 13 13 13 13 13 13 13 13 13 13 13
13 13 13 13 13 13 13 13 13 13 13 13 13 13 13 13
13 13 13 13 13 13 13 13 13 13 13 13 13 13 13 13
13 13 13 13 13 13 13 13 13 13 13 13 13 13 13 13
13 13 13 13 13 13 13 13 13 13 13 13 13 13 13 13

sun	street	tree	cat
yellow	beech	shadow	gazebo
snow	grass	shallow	glow
bee	blue	sky	avenue

14 14 14 14 14 14 14 14 14 14 14 14 14 14 14 14
14 14 14 14 14 14 14 14 14 14 14 14 14 14 14 14
14 14 14 14 14 14 14 14 14 14 14 14 14 14 14 14
14 14 14 14 14 14 14 14 14 14 14 14 14 14 14 14
14 14 14 14 14 14 14 14 14 14 14 14 14 14 14 14
14 14 14 14 14 14 14 14 14 14 14 14 14 14 14 14
14 14 14 14 14 14 14 14 14 14 14 14 14 14 14 14
14 14 14 14 14 14 14 14 14 14 14 14 14 14 14 14
14 14 14 14 14 14 14 14 14 14 14 14 14 14 14 14
14 14 14 14 14 14 14 14 14 14 14 14 14 14 14 14
14 14 14 14 14 14 14 14 14 14 14 14 14 14 14 14
14 14 14 14 14 14 14 14 14 14 14 14 14 14 14 14
14 14 14 14 14 14 14 14 14 14 14 14 14 14 14 14
14 14 14 14 14 14 14 14 14 14 14 14 14 14 14 14
14 14 14 14 14 14 14 14 14 14 14 14 14 14 14 14
14 14 14 14 14 14 14 14 14 14 14 14 14 14 14 14
14 14 14 14 14 14 14 14 14 14 14 14 14 14 14 14
14 14 14 14 14 14 14 14 14 14 14 14 14 14 14 14
14 14 14 14 14 14 14 14 14 14 14 14 14 14 14 14
14 14 14 14 14 14 14 14 14 14 14 14 14 14 14 14
14 14 14 14 14 14 14 14 14 14 14 14 14 14 14 14
14 14 14 14 14 14 14 14 14 14 14 14 14 14 14 14
14 14 14 14 14 14 14 14 14 14 14 14 14 14 14 14
14 14 14 14 14 14 14 14 14 14 14 14 14 14 14 14
14 14 14 14 14 14 14 14 14 14 14 14 14 14 14 14
14 14 14 14 14 14 14 14 14 14 14 14 14 14 14 14
14 14 14 14 14 14 14 14 14 14 14 14 14 14 14 14
14 14 14 14 14 14 14 14 14 14 14 14 14 14 14 14
14 14 14 14 14 14 14 14 14 14 14 14 14 14 14 14
14 14 14 14 14 14 14 14 14 14 14 14 14 14 14 14
14 14 14 14 14 14 14 14 14 14 14 14 14 14 14 14
14 14 14 14 14 14 14 14 14 14 14 14 14 14 14 14

boat	pain	goal	encroach
fail	rescue	daisy	groan

	Player One:
Number of words remembered:	
	Player Two:

14 14 14 14 14 14 14 14 14 14 14 14 14 14 14
14 14 14 14 14 14 14 14 14 14 14 14 14 14 14
14 14 14 14 14 14 14 14 14 14 14 14 14 14 14
14 14 14 14 14 14 14 14 14 14 14 14 14 14 14
14 14 14 14 14 14 14 14 14 14 14 14 14 14 14
14 14 14 14 14 14 14 14 14 14 14 14 14 14 14
14 14 14 14 14 14 14 14 14 14 14 14 14 14 14
14 14 14 14 14 14 14 14 14 14 14 14 14 14 14
14 14 14 14 14 14 14 14 14 14 14 14 14 14 14
14 14 14 14 14 14 14 14 14 14 14 14 14 14 14
14 14 14 14 14 14 14 14 14 14 14 14 14 14 14
14 14 14 14 14 14 14 14 14 14 14 14 14 14 14
14 14 14 14 14 14 14 14 14 14 14 14 14 14 14
14 14 14 14 14 14 14 14 14 14 14 14 14 14 14
14 14 14 14 14 14 14 14 14 14 14 14 14 14 14
14 14 14 14 14 14 14 14 14 14 14 14 14 14 14
14 14 14 14 14 14 14 14 14 14 14 14 14 14 14
14 14 14 14 14 14 14 14 14 14 14 14 14 14 14
14 14 14 14 14 14 14 14 14 14 14 14 14 14 14
14 14 14 14 14 14 14 14 14 14 14 14 14 14 14
14 14 14 14 14 14 14 14 14 14 14 14 14 14 14
14 14 14 14 14 14 14 14 14 14 14 14 14 14 14
14 14 14 14 14 14 14 14 14 14 14 14 14 14 14
14 14 14 14 14 14 14 14 14 14 14 14 14 14 14
14 14 14 14 14 14 14 14 14 14 14 14 14 14 14
14 14 14 14 14 14 14 14 14 14 14 14 14 14 14
14 14 14 14 14 14 14 14 14 14 14 14 14 14 14
14 14 14 14 14 14 14 14 14 14 14 14 14 14 14
14 14 14 14 14 14 14 14 14 14 14 14 14 14 14
14 14 14 14 14 14 14 14 14 14 14 14 14 14 14

Passage 1:
One day, there was some shallow snow on the green grass. (11)
The sky was deep blue. (5)
The yellow sun did glow. (5)
That snow did melt by my first class. (8)

Passage 2:
Ed and Mel's goal is to stop R. L. Nox. (10)
R. L. put a spell on them. (7)
He left with their parents. (5)
He put a spell on the people of Jalisp. (9)
He left with their stuff. (5)
He did attack the Felkin to get some gold. (9)
He did rob Caltrez. (4)
Now, R. L. wants the baby dragons. (7)
His plan is to be filthy rich. (7)

Passage 3:

There was a fox who did love potato chips. (9)

He often would look for a potato chip snack. (9)

He would find them by the picnic bench. (8)

He would not pass up a potato chip even if he did find it in the trash. (17)

One day a crow did land in the tree next to the fox. (13)

It held a bag of potato chips. (7)

The fox said, "Drop the bag for me." (8)

The crow didn't respond. (4)

The fox said to the crow, "I just don't want to miss your song. I must go in a bit." (20)

The crow did look at the fox. (7)

The fox sat to wait for a song. (8)

This did impress the crow. (5)

He began a song and did drop the bag. (9)

The fox had a yummy potato chip snack as he did follow the melody of the song. (17)

Passage 4:
To play softball, you need a softball, a bat, and a mitt. (12)
One kid will pitch the ball. (6)
One kid will bat the ball. (6)
One kid will catch the ball. (6)

Passage 5:
To paint a wall, you need paint, a paintbrush, and a wall. (12)
Dip the paintbrush into the paint. (6)
Don't let the paint drip. (5)
Brush the paint onto the wall with the paintbrush. (9)
Cover the wall with paint to finish the job. (9)

Note: If a student substitutes "landed in the tree" for "did land in the tree," do not count that as wrong. They are remembering the word with the corrected syntax for spoken language. You can count it as one word (landed) instead of two (did land) when tallying up the words remembered. If the student substitutes a completely different word, "flew into the tree" instead of "did land in the tree," help correct the student if you remember the correct wording.

Number of words remembered:	

Sentence Frame
Cut on dotted line to create a window to show only the new sentence to read.

15 15 15 15 15 15 15 15 15 15 15 15 15 15 15 15
15 15 15 15 15 15 15 15 15 15 15 15 15 15 15 15
15 15 15 15 15 15 15 15 15 15 15 15 15 15 15 15
15 15 15 15 15 15 15 15 15 15 15 15 15 15 15 15
15 15 15 15 15 15 15 15 15 15 15 15 15 15 15 15
15 15 15 15 15 15 15 15 15 15 15 15 15 15 15 15
15 15 15 15 15 15 15 15 15 15 15 15 15 15 15 15
15 15 15 15 15 15 15 15 15 15 15 15 15 15 15 15
15 15 15 15 15 15 15 15 15 15 15 15 15 15 15 15
15 15 15 15 15 15 15 15 15 15 15 15 15 15 15 15
15 15 15 15 15 15 15 15 15 15 15 15 15 15 15 15
15 15 15 15 15 15 15 15 15 15 15 15 15 15 15 15
15 15 15 15 15 15 15 15 15 15 15 15 15 15 15 15
15 15 15 15 15 15 15 15 15 15 15 15 15 15 15 15
15 15 15 15 15 15 15 15 15 15 15 15 15 15 15 15
15 15 15 15 15 15 15 15 15 15 15 15 15 15 15 15
15 15 15 15 15 15 15 15 15 15 15 15 15 15 15 15
15 15 15 15 15 15 15 15 15 15 15 15 15 15 15 15
15 15 15 15 15 15 15 15 15 15 15 15 15 15 15 15
15 15 15 15 15 15 15 15 15 15 15 15 15 15 15 15
15 15 15 15 15 15 15 15 15 15 15 15 15 15 15 15
15 15 15 15 15 15 15 15 15 15 15 15 15 15 15 15
15 15 15 15 15 15 15 15 15 15 15 15 15 15 15 15
15 15 15 15 15 15 15 15 15 15 15 15 15 15 15 15
15 15 15 15 15 15 15 15 15 15 15 15 15 15 15 15
15 15 15 15 15 15 15 15 15 15 15 15 15 15 15 15
15 15 15 15 15 15 15 15 15 15 15 15 15 15 15 15
15 15 15 15 15 15 15 15 15 15 15 15 15 15 15 15
15 15 15 15 15 15 15 15 15 15 15 15 15 15 15 15
15 15 15 15 15 15 15 15 15 15 15 15 15 15 15 15
15 15 15 15 15 15 15 15 15 15 15 15 15 15 15 15
15 15 15 15 15 15 15 15 15 15 15 15 15 15 15 15

Made in the USA
Las Vegas, NV
16 October 2024

96982117R00136